CW00801215

Serenity Rayne

- romance in blood -

Love you!

Rayne

PRINCESS LOST

HYBRID ROYALS - FIRE AND ICE

SERENITY RAYNE

Thank you to my family for understanding my drive to tell my stories.

Thank you to Second Look Author Services for being a true one stop shopping experience.

Thank you to KJ for helping with envisioning this world.

Thank you to Tash @ Dazed Designs for making my vision of these covers come to life.

ALSO BY SERENITY RAYNE

Ascend Little Wolf

Hunt Little Wolf

Fight Little Wolf

Attack Little Wolf

Welcome Home Little Wolf

A Very Klaus Christmas

Edgar Allan Poe Retellings

Once Upon A Raven

Heart Shaped Box: A Tell-Tale Heart Retelling

MUSICAL INSPIRATION PROVIDED BY:

Fall Out Boy - My Songs Know What You Did in
the Dark

Tchaikowski - Swan Lake

Debussy - Claire De Lune

ADULT SUPERVISION REQUIRED

Fated Mates
Slow Burn
Sexual Tension
Hidden Enemies

PROLOGUE

AURORA

Oberon appears in a shimmering mist not far from where Tiamat had crash landed. "You need time to grow young one. The mind must catch up with your body." He says musically as his glowing hand touches the temple of Tiamat's dragon.

His eyes turn to me and he bows his head. "Young Queen, I must confess, I did not foresee the resurrection of the Blood Queen's line in your daughter." His eyes drop as his lithe hand glides over Tia's scales.

"What do you mean resurrection? What have you done my King?" Alaric asks, trying to reign in his temper. My eyes dart over to my mate as he dares to question the Fae King.

Oberon keeps his glowing hand upon Tia's temple, slowly his lavender eyes lock with Alaric's. "The world needs a protector, a guardian besides your mate. Which, I must admit, we engineered her birth as well." Oberon narrows his eyes in thought for a moment.

I'm shocked to the core to learn that I was engineered by the Fae as a weapon. Alaric's and Nicodeamus' tempers radiate from them like the waves of the ocean. "So my mate died so you could create a hybrid so you could bring back the Blood Queen?" Nico says through gritted teeth. Both of my brows shoot up at my father's revelation.

"Essentially, yes." Oberon says with a scary finality. "Though this knowledge will not be yours after I leave. The only one to remember will be Aurora. She must protect Tiamat at all costs." Oberon's lavender gaze moves to me and he tilts his head studying me closely.

"You cannot tell anyone of the future your daughter holds. Just like her knowledge of her mate's location will be hidden from her till the time is right." Oberon slowly removes his hand from Tia's dragon's temple. "She must sleep through each of her heat cycles till her twenty-fourth birthday, after that I will make it possible for her to locate her mate."

His head turns till he looks at Alaric, Nicodeamus and Ladon. "Sleep and forget all that you learned here today. You must keep the Princess pure and strong till she meets her mate. Protect her at all costs." Oberon says and waves his hand, as his hand passes each male they crumple to the ground fast asleep. It was a very surreal: *these are not the droids you're looking for* moment. "I do not envy the burden you now carry young Queen, guard your secrets well." Oberon says before disappearing in a shimmer of glitter.

I stand there up to my knees in snow gobsmacked by the information relayed to me. My precious daughter will be stronger than all of us combined. I walk over and lightly run my hands over Tia's scales. Not long after Oberon's departure the guys slowly start to awaken and hold their heads. Protective details are created each day as a different family member will stay with Tia till it was safe to awaken her.

~Five years later~

STANDING on my balcony I look out over the private gardens of the Summer Chalet. It's summer and the various flowers are in full bloom filling the air with a myriad of wonderful scents. In the center of the garden my precious Tia is fencing with her Grandfather, Nicodeamus. My father is a well renowned swordsman and for him to be training my daughter is a blessing. My mate stands on the sidelines already defeated by his daughter earlier. Tia is pound for pound the most lethal of us all, you can show her something once and she knows it. My father finally disarms her after almost two hours of intensive battle. They smile and laugh, then hug it out. I can hear my father explaining to her where she left herself open and how to correct it.

Tia nods slowly taking in all of the information relayed to her, and she smiles looking at her brother trying to taunt him. Ladon eventually nods and grabs his father's sword and faces off against his sister. Tia plays with Ladon, she smacks him on the ass with her practice sword and literally runs circles around him just for fun. Quickly she disarms him after her father tells her to stop messing with her brother.

Tia smiles and hugs her brother, kissing his cheek. She then tells him what he did wrong and makes him walk back through the final moves again. Alaric and Nicodeamus stand shoulder to shoulder watching the twins. Part of me feels as if I am neglecting the other children's training. I feel so guilty carrying the burden of the truth and keeping it from everyone. In my heart of hearts I know I've done the right thing, but to carry the truth alone weighs heavy on me.

~Ten years after~

ONE OF MY favorite songs echoes through the Alpha house and rouses me from my slumber. I walk out into the main meeting hall and there are my children playing music. Tia has her lead guitar in her hand and starts the opening chords to *Fall Out Boy's* - *"My Songs Know What You Did in the Dark."* Ladon also has his lead guitar, Kirra has her bass, and Jayce is on the drums playing his heart out. The kids play in perfect harmony and Tia sings with such emotion. The Alpha house starts to fill with our pack members as the song progresses. Every-time the part where they say *light'em up*, Tia lets go of her guitar, flips her hands, with her palms facing up and her frost flames rise up from her hands. The stronger she pronounces the word *fire* the higher and brighter the flames become. It gets to the point that Ladon takes over playing the lead guitar parts for her.

Tiamat's eyes begin to glow with the flames as she ends up just holding the flames in her hands in front of her. I'm almost hypnotized by Tia's power and control. Then I remember what Oberon told me about my daughter. I draw in a deep breath knowing that I am witnessing the tip of the proverbial iceberg with Tia. The song finally comes to an end and Tia is still holding her frost flames. I watch Ladon come up alongside her and she extinguishes one of her hands to cup his. Their eyes glow a faint blue and soon the flames rise up in Ladon's hand that Tia is holding. She smiles and motions to his free hand and he reproduces flames in that hand. Tia closes her hands soon after, extinguishing the flames, and Ladon follows suit, then they hug it out afterwards.

"What was that about? And since when can she do that?" Alaric asks me, whispering in my ear.

"She's her father's daughter, powerful and ready for anything." I say hoping to stroke Alaric's ego to the point he drops the subject. He smiles broadly and nods. He kisses my temple then grabs Ladon to go visit with Gisella and Austin for a few days. Ladon is considering going to their Kingdom to train in their style of fighting. Tia wants to go with them but Alaric forbids her since there are so many virile males in the Stormbringer Kingdom. Tia is livid about always being left behind. To make it up to her, I call for a girls day at the spa just to make her feel special again. I wish I could tell her why.

~19 years after~

IT'S the night of the twins' twenty-fourth birthday celebration in the Winter Palace. Ladon is schmoozing with any female that has a heartbeat. Tia on the other hand keeps refusing suitors advances because her dragoness gets angry. I watch as Tia's eyes faintly glow and Dante is at her side in a moment. I know she wishes to dance but she doesn't trust most of the guests to respect her boundaries. Tia and Dante look to me before he extends his hand to her. I smile and nod allowing them to share a dance. Tia has a crush on Dante because of his rugged good looks and his bad boy aura.

That man has been her best friend and confidant since Oberon's truth bomb detonated. I only shared the truth with Dante and Edgar since she seems to favor them the most. The honest to Goddess truth is that I know it's because Luna has a major crush on Marco, who unbeknownst to her, is her true mate. Tia and Dante laugh and carry on as they twirl and dance around the hall. I can't help but smile watching how happy my daughter is. "Mom?" Ladon says as he moves to sit next to me.

"Yes?" Ladon looks puzzled watching his sister. "It sucks that Draven and his parents couldn't make it, damn border disputes." He says with a tinge of anger in his voice. He knows that matters of state take prescient over frivolities.

"It does suck, but your father and you are flying there tomorrow to assist. Marco is bringing a group of about nine Black Dragons with you." I raise a knowing eyebrow at my son. I've heard of some of the scandalous things the two of them have gotten themselves into.

Ladon smiles then leaves to go back to chasing the young dragoness' that are hoping to be his mate. Tia returns to my side smiling after dancing with both Dante and Edgar. "One day Mom, I want nothing more than to share a dance with my mate." A single tear attempts to roll down her cheek but freezes before it gets too far. You can clearly hear the pain in her voice and feel it ebb from her pores.

"You will love, you will. Just be patient I'm sure Prince Charming is just as anxious to find you as well. Besides these balls give you the chance to see most of the eligible bachelors." I watch Tia nod her head slowly as she returns her gaze back to the dance floor. Several new males enter the ballroom and yet none catch her eye. I know none of these males stand a chance. My gut tells me I know who the lucky male is, but my mind gets foggy when I think about it too hard. Damn Oberon.

Speaking of the Devil, Oberon arrives and glides his way over to us. "My Queen, Princess, happy birthday to you and your twin. Tis a wonderful night for a celebration." He says musically. His lavender eyes glow faintly for a moment before he speaks again. "If you can have one thing in the entire world Princess, what would it be?" He asks with a mischievous look in his eye.

"I'll be honest M'lord, I wish to find my mate." Tia says in a sigh. She folds her hands tightly in her lap before making eye contact with Oberon. "I wish for a good hearted male like my Daddy Jayce, one as powerful as my birth father. He needs to be as strong and gentle as Papa Bear, and as wise as Daddy Arnulf and Daddy Dominik. I hope he's as playful as Daddy Klaus." She sighs again looking down now at her hands. "It's an impossible wish list is it not?" She questions softly.

Oberon reaches out and cups Tia's cheek and smiles looking at her. "Not impossible Princess, good men exist, you just have to look for them." His hand and eyes glow faintly, if I'm not mistaken he just gave her the ability to find her mate. "Dream of your mate Princess and perhaps someday soon you will be presented with your future." He says with a smile then kisses her forehead before disappearing in a puff of glitter.

"Do you think he speaks truly mother?" Tia asks and I can see hope blossoming in her gray-blue eyes.

"I believe so hatchling, say your prayers, wish on the dragon star, and who knows. Your wish may just come true." I say smiling broadly, I'm anxious to see who fate decided to gift my daughter with as a mate.

ONE

TIAMAT

EVERY NIGHT IS THE SAME. THE DREAMS START OFF in a flower-filled field on a hill overlooking my father's kingdom. A light breeze blows through the air moving the flowers in a gentle sway from left to right in slow motion. Tall lush green grass in the surrounding area moves like waves on the ocean rippling across the land. The pale blue sky above is so cloudless and vibrant, perfectly clear ethereal blue, making it excellent for flying. But in these dreams I never do.

I stand and begin walking leisurely towards the pond my fathers' like taking me to. Fond memories of my child-hood flow through my mind remembering the good times we had. Like the time Dad was teaching Ladon and I to hunt. I make it to the pond and just like all the times before, there's a man standing hip deep in the shallow waters facing away from me.

He has dark brown almost black hair, styled where the hair on top is long and the sides are shaved tightly close to his scalp. On his right shoulder he has an intricate tribal tattoo that appears to be either Samoan or Mayan in design. It's made of thick black lines and delicate details around the edges. It starts on his trapezius muscle and flows all the way to his elbow, woven in and out of the main design. His skin is a delicious golden brown and the muscles across his broad back and shoulders are well defined. He is Adonis made flesh. My dragoness whines begging us to will him to turn around, just once so we can see what he looks like. This man, this God has haunted my every dream since I came of age. Twenty years of these torturous dreams, wondering who he is.

"Please turn. Please look at me!" I implore him every night. And every night ends with the same result. He starts to turn and moments before it happens, I wake up. Every. Damn. Time. Tonight, this torturous dream is the same. Just as he turns I wake up. It's becoming emotionally draining to endure the same dream night after night. Though it seems as if the dreams have become more detailed since my twenty-fourth birthday. Previously I could make out the man's form but it was blurry. Now, I see him as if he's standing before me. I can almost feel what direction he's in, but it's not solid enough to follow. Almost like a faint tugging in a general direction.

I SIT UP, tears flowing freely down my cheeks. So close yet so far away. I can almost feel him as if I almost know where he is. My heart aches to the point I rub my chest over my sternum. A quick knock sounds at my door, and I sigh already knowing who it is.

"Come in mother." I adjust my nightgown and watch my mother close the door softly behind her.

"Are you okay, Tia?" She asks, as she comes and sits next to me threading her fingers through the tangles in my long pale blonde hair.

"As okay as I'm gonna be, mother," I answer her as tears begin to roll down my cheeks as my heartache makes itself known.

"What is wrong with me? Why do I keep seeing him?" I ask, staring into my mother's pale grey eyes.

Mother embraces me and her beast rumbles softly trying to soothe me. I sigh softly nuzzling my mother's cheek. "He's your mate baby girl," Mom laughs softly. "I dreamt of most of my mates before my ascension, too," Mom pulls back and looks into my eyes again.

"Will I ascend too?" I look curiously into my mother's eyes.

"I'm honestly not sure, little one," Mother smiles at me and kisses my temple.

"But what I do know is it's time we start looking for your mate. Do you know what species he is?" Mother tilts her head left, right then back to the middle again looking at me curiously.

I lower my head and shake it side to side. "I know he can wield lighting, I can feel his flames as if they are my own."

I manifest my frost flames in my hand staring at them. The blue and white flames flicker and lick wildly in my hand. "Other than that I have no idea what he is. Or more importantly, who he is," Snuffing out the flames I drop my hands to my lap, feeling defeated, almost broken by the idea I may never find him. "I think he's like me, you know, more than one species." I add, as I gently wipe away a tear that managed to roll down my cheek.

"No time to mope Tiamat! Your father and grandfather have lived far longer than I have." Mom begins to tap her chin as she starts planning. "Maybe they can start inviting eligible bachelors that are of age here to meet you this summer." Mother smiles at me and the eyes of her beast blaze to the forefront.

"We will find him even if I have to rip this world to shreds to do it." I watch as my mother shifts her right arm to her taloned gauntlet and slices open her palm on her left hand. Taking the hint I follow suit and shift my right arm to my taloned gauntlet and slice my left palm open. We press our hands together and hold them firmly, our taloned hands surrounding the flesh ones. "With my blood, this I swear." My mother says swearing a blood oath with me.

My bedroom door blasts open with my father Alaric and my other dad's hot on his heels. They stare concerned at the scene before them. Slowly we raise our taloned gauntlets at the same time, frost passing between them in a mini snowstorm with mini-arcs of lightning. Our beast's eyes locked together, I share my vision and dreams with my mother so she can see whom I'm so desperately searching for.

Moments pass, and mother gasps, releasing my hand, and a slow smile creeping across her ruby red lips. "Alaric, reach out to all the royal houses, any who bore sons with fire and lightning. Invite them, we will have them visit and see if any click with our baby." Mom stands up, placing both hands on her hips staring at her mates. I have to laugh watching my fathers' cringe because of the look mom is giving them.

"As you wish my love." My birth father Alaric is the first to approach mom and kiss her temple. "There's only two houses that bear the weapons you describe.The Storm-bringers another royal house and the Illisuans." Alaric strokes his beard. "I know the parents of both houses, and I have an invitation to the Stormbringers annual Tourna-ment. I can inquire while we're there."

"Tia?" Father says, releasing mom and heads towards me. Dad grabs my hands and smiles looking down at me. "You're only twenty-five, baby girl. Are you sure this is what you want?"

Mom promptly smacks him upside the back of his head. I can barely contain my laughter as I nod slowly. "Yes Daddy, this is what I want." I stand up and lay my head on his chest seeking comfort from him.

· · ·

EVENTUALLY, my twin comes in and looks at the gathering. "What did I miss? You okay sis?" Ladon tilts his head as he looks at me. I know deep down he felt my anguish, but he's trying to be the tough guy and not show that he actually cares about his sister.

"I'll be ok Ladon," I sigh and force myself to smile as I pull away from Dad.

I move away from our father and rush over, hugging my brother tightly, nuzzling his shoulder and neck. Looking up at Ladon, "I'm going to miss you while you're off training." Forcing a smile on my face. "Maybe I'll come with Mom and Dad when they go to the dragon trials ceremony so I can see you."

I'm so proud of my brother, he was accepted to train the elite Dragon Enforcers in the Bronze Dragon court. I'm going to miss the hell out of him. Just thinking about it causes my eyes to well up with tears again. Blinking, a few tears start to slowly fall and roll down my cheek. This will be the first time we've been separated for more than a day or two.

Ladon's dragon starts to rumble trying to soothe me and my dragoness. I feel like my heart is breaking all over again. First I can't find my mate and now my brother is leaving me for up to a year.

"Shh Tia. It's ok sissy.." He gently runs his fingers through my hair. "It's not like you can't fly and see me, or walk in the astral plane to get to me," Ladon says, trying to sooth me and settle my nerves.

"I know little brother, we've never been apart long." I say softly as I hug him tightly.

Ladon nuzzles my cheek and kisses my temple, "I love you, Tia." He says cupping my cheek. "Distance will never change a brother's love for his sister." He says with such determination.

I rise up on tippy toes and kiss Ladon's cheek. "Love you too Ladon, with all my heart."

Ladon takes my hand and rests it over his heart. "You are always in my heart Tia, we can feel each other's pain and distress. I will always be here for you no matter where life takes me."

We press our foreheads together and coat each other in our frost. Our dragons' croon to each other comforting one another the only way they know how. Someone blowing their nose breaks us out of our little bubble. We look up to see Mom crying and our Dads' all touching her while our birth father holds her tightly.

Out of all of their children, we are the closest and the most attached to each other. From day one we took care of each other and always will. I'm scared of Ladon leaving, *what if something happens? What if he needs me and I'm too far away?* I'm not used to being without him, and maybe it's just anxiety on my part. But, then again he may find his mate on his journey and I'll gain another sister.

Ladon kisses my temple once more then goes to mom and hugs her before leaving. Our fathers' follow Ladon out as I head to my closet to get dressed for the day.

MY DADS' always fill my closet with some of the most beautiful dresses they can find. I guess you can call them light summer dresses ranging in length from knee length to floor length. Looking at my closet, it looks like a rainbow puked in every pastel shade humanly possible. Scanning through the rack, I pick my favorite pink sundress and grab my art supplies and head out of my room.

"M'lady?" Dante calls to me from his post near my room. I smile and slightly bow my head to him as he takes the art supplies from me. "Where are we off to today?"

I ponder his question then smile up at him, "Appletree Hill and then Mirror Lake if it's not too much trouble." I mention the locations from my dreams, secretly I'm hoping one of these times my mate will be there.

Dante smiles then bows at his waist, "anything you wish, princess. You are so much easier to protect than your Momma is." He has that mischievous gleam in his eye.

"Who drew the short straw this time?" I try to keep from laughing, poor guys' draw straws over whose turn it is to protect my mother.

"Marco..." Dante bursts out laughing, like a full-on belly laugh. Marco is a big slow Black Dragon, the poor man has a hard time keeping up with my mother.

"Oh, geez...Poor guy." We head out into the courtyard of the Ice Dragon Castle to the launching area. I catch sight of my brother flying off into the distance and wish him a safe journey.

"Princess?" Dante says snapping his fingers to pull me from my thoughts, then swirls his finger around, making the turn around motion with his hand. I turn my back to him as he strips and shifts. Father wishes for me to be kept as innocent for as long as possible.

Dante's dragon taps its talons to let me know he's ready. I walk over and gather up his clothing and place them in the satchel along with my art supplies. After everything is stowed away I walk to Dante's taloned hand and he grips the bag then lays down for me to climb on. His War Dragon is built like a flying tank, thick armored bronze scales, and large horns upon his head.

I find a comfortable place behind Dante's crown of horns and sit down ready for our flight. My father's birth kingdom is beautiful and one day it will be all mine to rule. We call it the Land of Eternal Winter. This particular region of Siberia rarely thaws, most of the year it's covered in some form of ice or snow. Thankfully we've almost had a summer here for the last five years. I get to see the native flowers and fields of a lush green. Don't get me wrong, I love winter. But I also love the colors of the wild flowers.

Come to think of it, I'm kind of jealous of my other siblings: only myself, Ladon, and Kirra will ever hold a title. Since mother and father believe that a Monarchy led by a strong Queen is the way to go. Poor Ladon will only rule if something happens to me or if I decide to abdicate the throne. Kirra stands to inherit the Marelup Castle when she takes a mate. My Bear and Dire Wolf siblings have nothing they need to live up to. It must be nice to just live, not have the weight of the world on their shoulders.

WE ARRIVE QUICKER than I anticipated and land in the field near the tree that starts my dream. The lush green grass comes up to Dante's dragon's wrists and sways gently in the strong breeze. I slide off of Dante's back and pull his clothing out of my satchel.

I walk towards the tree and look out across the rolling hills watching the flowers and grass move like water. There's a myriad of colors of wild flowers this year that dot the countryside bringing a beautiful range of colors. I stand there for what feels like forever before I swing my satchel up on my shoulder and start walking towards the lake.

It only takes me fifteen minutes to retrace my steps to the lake. The earth is soft and wet under my bare feet. I love the way the earth moves as I step upon it. I walk the edge of the lake until I get to the exact place where the man of my dreams usually appears.

I look over my shoulder and spot Dante sitting on a log not too far away. Carefully, I set up my art supplies and draw in a deep breath and close my eyes. I go back to my dream and conjure the man I call my personal incubi.

Once I have his form fresh in my mind I start to paint him in intricate and intimate detail. Every line of muscle and sinew is defined and shaded properly. My brush strokes caress every ripple of muscle and the cut of his waist. His firm muscular ass, damn I want to sink my canines into that blessing of an ass. Between that ass and his thick shoulders, there is definitely a promise of power. His ink, Gods save me. I want to lick every curve, line, and detail.

For some reason now that I am painting him, I can feel his power, his fire. Its warmth reaches me as if he is standing before me. I want to touch it. I want to bathe in his flames. I paint his hand upturned and even with his hip. In his hand I place brilliant streaks of lightning and red flames flickering. I stare at my Adonis and sigh softly, gently running my fingers over his form.

I wish I could see him. Just for once I wish selfishly for something for myself. I wish I knew where my mate was. I can only hope that mom and dad can find him. It has to be him, no one else will do.

TWO

DRAVEN

I WAKE UP IN A SWEAT-SOAKED BED ONCE
again...will it ever end? I run my fingers through my hair
frustrated beyond belief. I want to know why she stalks
me in my dreams and torments me. In the last year the
dreams are clearer and more frequent. But, yet still feel
incomplete. I've kicked off my covers as if I've literally
chased her. Rubbing my face, I close my eyes and I
remember the dream like I do every night.

The woman has long blonde wavy hair, porcelain skin,
and legs for days. She is always in a flowing pink dress
facing away from me. It's adorable that I find her every
night without shoes.

Her crescent moon tattoo on her right wrist is the only
real detail I get to see clearly. Every time I reach out for
her she takes off running into the woods, her hair whip-
ping behind her, giggling the most melodic sound I've
ever heard. Frost trails behind her as she disappears from

my sight. She stirs my dragon to the core making me yell out mid-shift and that's it.

I want to know who she is and why my dreams always take me to her. I've had the dream since I was eight and fully matured over night. I've kept the dreams a secret from everyone, even my siblings.

At twenty-eight years old, I can't take it anymore. It's time to go ask mom.. Mother and father wish to arrange a political marriage with another noble house for me this summer. Hopefully I can find whomever this mystery maiden is before then. I need to speak with my parents post haste.

AS QUICKLY AS I CAN, I get dressed and leave my room. I make my way through my parent's side of the castle quickly and knock on their door. Luckily for me, everyone is already awake and having coffee from what I can smell. I knock firmly on the large red cedar door to their bedroom.

"Good morning, son." My father says as he opens the door with one arm wide open, inviting me in. He moves off to the side giving me room to enter.

"Morning, dad. Is mom here or is she out on a flight?" I ask looking around the room. Hoping to find my mom quickly.

"She is getting out of the shower," he says with a lovesick smirk.

Austin Skybane, once the greatest fighter, now King Consort of the Bronze Dragon court. Dad is a little over six foot tall and if I had to guess he's about two hundred pounds. Of solid muscle, lucky for me I'm built heavier than my dad. But, I did get his speed and agility and his black hair.

I chuckle at him and take a seat on the benched window sill. One day, I want a love like theirs. It doesn't phase me at all that they are so open about their relationship. I hope that one day I can find a love like theirs. She's out there, I've been seeing her in my dreams for twenty years.

"Good morning, son," my mother's voice is like smooth silk coating my nerves. She has a way of keeping me relaxed when I'm stressed out. Mom seems to glide over the floor as she heads towards me.

"Morning!" I say with a huge smile on my face, going to hug her tightly but quick. Gisella Stormbringer, Queen of the Bronze Dragons. I wish I had gotten mom's ash brown hair, instead I got her wavy locks. If I had to describe my mom, besides powerful, I'd say she reminds me of a cross between a certain Amazon and a dancer.

My mom always makes me laugh when she zaps my poor father playfully with her lightning. Father being a Gold Dragon always calls forth his flames to taunt mother in retaliation.

Mother quickly turns her focus back on me. "What is troubling you, sweetheart? I can feel the tension rolling off of you like waves in an angry sea." The concern in her eyes is touching. Being her firstborn, she knows me better than I know myself sometimes. She pulls me over to the chest at the foot of the bed and we sit with our hands overlapping.

"I don't know if going through with the political marriage you suggested is a good idea." I say dropping my shoulders and lowering my gaze looking down at the floor. "There's something I have to tell you. Something I have kept to myself for a very long time and I am terrified of how this might change things." I say on a sigh, it's probably one of the toughest secrets I've kept. Every inch of my body is tense as I am about to tell them my biggest secret.

"Sweetheart, it's okay. You can tell us anything." Mother smiles at me and father nods in agreement. Mother reaches out and gently caresses my cheek trying to get me to look at her.

Taking a deep breath I finally look up at them both quickly before pouring my heart out. "I keep seeing this beautiful woman in my dreams." Smiling, I sigh wistfully. "I've been seeing her every night since I was eight." Quickly I release my mother's hands and then grip the hem of my shirt.

"I see her back but never her face to identify her. She is absolutely stunning," I say getting lost in my description of her. "Her hair is a very pale blonde almost white, her skin almost ivory in color." My voice has a soft almost gentle quality to it. I want nothing more than to hold my mate in my arms

"She always takes off into the forest with a giggle and frost left behind her. Everything she touches freezes almost immediately. I've never seen anyone like her." My eyes move between my mother and father anxiously. "It's as if she is the living embodiment of the Goddess Skadi, the Goddess of Winter." My tone is filled with wonder as I ponder the ramifications of the parallels.

"She taunts me every night, and all I want to do is hunt her down and make her mine. My Drake is itching to hunt for her, but I know I have an obligation to our kingdom and to you both." Feeling defeated, my shoulders lower and I drop my gaze again.

"I don't want to disappoint you guys or cause any political unrest. The kingdom expects the announcement of my betrothal by summer." I say exasperated, placing my elbows on my knees and burying my face in my hands.

"Look, I know it's not easy, Draven." My father lays his hands on my shoulders attempting to comfort me. "Love is often a hard road and it's not perfect. You've seen how all of us operate and maybe that will be true for you too, son," my father interjects.

"I only want her though, no offense," I say quickly. "I have been waiting to find her, she calls to my soul every night in my dreams." Roughly I run my hands through my hair in frustration.

"I understand," mom says. "If you cannot find your dream mate before the summer then you will need to go through with an arranged marriage." Mother looks as defeated as I feel.

"We have all made promises that we must keep. I wish you would have told us sooner, Draven." Father says sympathetically.

"I know, but I didn't want to let anyone down. It's my duty as firstborn to ascend to the throne and marry first." I say with conviction. In all honesty, the idea of marrying because of duty makes me sick to my stomach when I know my mate is out there somewhere.

"Yes, but son, you must marry for your heart as well," my father says kindly. He gives me a wink and I pick up on what he's trying to convey.

"You mentioned ice and frost, there's only three royal houses that have that weapon. Kraus, Dimeter and Wolferson, perhaps I can inquire if they have daughters for you to meet?" My father offers. "Then again I did send an invitation to the Kraus kingdom, Alaric is a close personal friend of mine."

Finally I have a spark of hope that my mate may be found. "Ladon comes from the Kraus family and I know he has a sister." I know Ladon has pale blonde hair and if I remember right his sister had the same color. "Brighton comes from Wolferson and he has a sister." I ponder the third house named. "Riley has three sisters, though from what I hear they are terrors." I roll my eyes dramatically which causes my father to laugh.

We embrace in a hug, "I'll see you two in the hall for

lunch later." I turn and leave their room feeling much lighter about my situation.

NOW TO GET a hold of Ladon and tell him about my predicament. We've been friends for as long as I can remember. I can't wait for him to get here and train with the teams. There is so much we can learn from him and he can learn a lot from us as well.

I feel my skin ripple with my scales just under the surface. I need to go fly or train for a bit until this room of mine airs out from my pheromones. I take a quick shower, dress in my work out gear with my hair tied up and grab my gym bag. The faster I can get out of this wing of the castle the better.

I grab my phone and send Ladon a quick goofy selfie. My damn hair is all over the place and I honestly don't give a fuck at the moment. I'm sure he is laughing like a hyena right about now. I don't wait for a response, Instead I throw my phone into my bag and get ready for training with pops. For over seven hundred and eighty years old, the man is in top condition. There are many reasons why he was king...his knack for strategy being number one on the list.

"Hello, Draven," Pops says as I enter the training pit.

"Hey, Pops. How are you doing today?" I say as I drop my bag and put on my arm guards.

"The sun is bright and all is good in the kingdom. It is a glorious day, my boy. Now, tell me, what's troubling you? You normally don't ask me to train with you," he says, getting straight to the point. Pop's stretches several times and starts to circle me. Slowly he's leaving footprints in the sand of the pit.

"I have a lot to learn from you and I would like to ask for your wisdom." Tilting my head to the side, my eyes follow Pop's as he circles me like a vulture. At hearing that, we start to fight as boxers do. The level we are on under the castle is enchanted by the mages to absorb any shock to the castle, it's a safe place to spar.

"Did you think you would ever find your true mate?" I inquire as we trade blows.

"I never thought I would be so lucky. Like you, my parents thought a betrothal was a grand idea." Pops rolls his eyes dramatically and shakes his head slowly. "I wanted to match with a few different ladies in my time before your Grams, but my heart was never truly happy until I saw her." My grandfather says wistfully.

"What was it like when you met?" I ask curiously, Pop's has definitely piqued my curiosity.

"Draven, it's not like you to ask me questions such as these. Have you spoken to your parents?" He asks just before he crosses his arms over his chest.

"Definitely, they are reaching out to a select few Royal houses as we speak." I smile broadly, as I look towards the stairs.

"Then that is all that you need," he says before landing a punch to my ribs, knocking me slightly breathless. The old man still knows how to land a hit.

I hear a roar, announcing the arrival of someone. It can't be Ladon, I messaged him not long ago! The sneaky devil got here early. Pops nods to me and I nod back knowing it's okay to leave. I grab my things and rush upstairs to greet my best friend.

~Ladon~

I ROAR my greeting into the wind so the guards don't attempt to roast my ass. I circle the castle grounds making lazy circles in the air enjoying the thermals. I enjoy looking at the architecture of Draven's family's castle. It's so different from the Winter Palace or even the Summer Chalet.

The masonry is much newer than any of my family's castles, it's very modern in comparison. Just like at home there's lush gardens inside and outside the castle walls. Just outside the gates there's a field large enough for my dragon to land. Carefully, I drop my two bags and then come in for the landing.

Tilting my head back I roar once more before shifting back to my human form and dress quickly. I wait patiently for Draven to come out to greet me so that I can easily gain entrance to the castle. It's now that I notice that my phone is making noises in my bag. Digging through all my clothes I finally find my phone and laugh at the picture Draven sent me.

"Ladon, you shit! Why didn't you tell me you were coming early?" Draven says with a laugh as he comes running over to me.

I roll my eyes and move forward to bro-hug him. "Fuck you too my friend so much for a hey it's awesome you're here early!" I can't help but smirk at him and shake my head.

"It is awesome that you're here early, man. I was just sparing with pops when I heard your call. Are you ready for training here?" Draven asks, punching me in the shoulder. I watch his nose twitch several times then stop.

"Hell yeah I am! I've been sparring with all manner of beings for years. The only person I can't beat is Tiamat." I hang my head in shame for a moment. "Her frost and ice is much more powerful than mine." My eyes widen as I remember I promised Tia I'd let her know I arrived safely.

"Shit, that reminds me I have to let her know I got here okay otherwise she'll kill me." I fire off a quick text to my twin and take a quick selfie with the castle in the background and send it to her as well. "So? What do you want to do first?" I ask him as I look around.

"First we eat, I'm starving. Then we get to formulating tactical plans for how we can kick some serious ass in this tournament," Draven says smirking with an evil look to his eyes.

"Sounds like a plan." I walk over and grab my bags and sling them over my shoulder. Several dings go off in succession, I stop walking and look at my messages quickly. I can't help but laugh at Tia sending me a shopping list and a selfie. My silly sister actually did her makeup and painted her lips blood red like mom's. She's almost a carbon copy but we both got pale blonde hair. Her note says to say hi to everyone for her.

THE WIND CHANGES direction suddenly blowing some of my hair in my face, quickly I move it out of the way. Draven zones out staring off into the distance transfixed by something I can't find for the life of me. I watch his scales ripple along his skin then he swipes at his nose and comes back from wherever he just was.

"You ok man? You spaced out on me." I stare at him concerned. "Did you see that my sister Tia says hi to everyone?" I wave her picture and message in his face again.

"I'm good bro, just caught a whiff of something that caught my attention." Draven's eyes widen and his eyebrows raise in shock. "Whoa! That's Tia?" I watch his pupils expand and contract quickly. "The little girl that had all those ringlets as a child, is that her?" He raises his eyebrows. "Wow, did she grow up fast, she's beautiful!" Draven says more to himself than to me.

"Yeah, technically she's about five minutes older than me. But she didn't stay in her dragon form as long as I did." I shrug my shoulders like it's no big deal. "I wanted to grow up faster so that I could fight and train. She wanted to enjoy her time and grow up slowly." I roll my eyes and look back at Draven.

"What scent did you catch? I don't smell anything out of the ordinary." I sniff my shirt and roll my eyes. "Damn Tia scent marked me again. I gotta change and shower I smell like my freaking sister. No female will want to come near me smelling like this," I say in a huff pulling at my shirt. "She's always doing that shit to me!" I say in mock anger.

"I'm sorry, she did what?" Draven's eyebrows shoot up. "She left her scent all over you? Gross man." He wrinkles his nose looking at me." Go shower *before* we eat," Draven says laughing at me.

"I really don't know what I smelled to be honest but I am determined to find out." Draven shrugs his shoulders slowly. "It's the shit my dreams are made of." Draven sighs softly then looks in the direction the wind had come from before. I can only guess he's hoping to smell whatever caught his attention before, again.

"I know one thing. My sister smells better than your room probably does." I sit my bags down and take my shirt off and throw it in Draven's face. I start laughing at Draven as I rub my wrists before picking up my bags again.

As I start walking towards the castle I stop when I don't hear Draven walking behind me. I turn around and yell for him as he is transfixed by my shirt. "Bro, are you okay, Draven? Not falling in love with my shirt are you?" I raise an eyebrow looking at him.

"No you ass," he says, shaking his head. I catch his eyes drifting to my shirt then back again to me before he starts moving again.

I'm not so convinced that he is okay. Something has changed about him and I'll get to the bottom of it, quick. He's definitely acting odd even for him. "Mind showing me to my room so I can shower?"

"Yeah, let's get going before any of the cortisones show up and want to tag along!" Draven says laughing walking next to me towards the castle.

WALKING through the castle I am greeted by the people and guards alike. It is truly a magnificent castle. I study the architecture as well as the artwork on the walls. My twin got me interested in oil paintings and frescoes so now, unfortunately, I look for them. I take several pictures and send them to Tia. We walk in silence to the wing where Draven and his family stay.

"Here you go, room de Draven," he says, opening the large golden oak door for me.

"You are staying in the room next door to me. I figured you wouldn't want to be on the far side of the castle." He says, gesturing me towards the room.

"Good enough for me," I say, placing my hand on his shoulder and head to the luxurious bathroom ahead of me. I take a fast shower just to get the grime from traveling off my skin. When I am done I head out with a towel around my waist and one I'm using to dry my hair. "Tell me again, why did you agree to a possible arranged marriage?" I inquire and take a seat nearby.

"Because it will strengthen family ties with one of the other great dragon bloodlines. My parents asked me and I was inclined to agree," Draven shrugs his shoulders.

"I will do what's best for the kingdom, even if it means being in a loveless relationship with a woman I have no interest in," He says, sounding defeated while surveying the room.

I sigh softly and look out the window for a moment. "Tia is in a similar situation, Dad wants to marry her off to strengthen an alliance. Sometimes I'm thankful I'm second born." Shrugging my shoulders I slowly turn to face Draven again. "That's true loyalty, I commend both of you for that." Tilting my head to the side I watch him carefully. "What if you find your mate?" I prompt curiously.

"That's what I need to talk to you about," he says quietly as he fidgets with his hands. Draven searches the room for what I can only assume is listening devices. This is that important to him to keep it a secret and I will keep it that. We've been friends for so long that we are more brothers than friends. Hell, I'm closer to Draven than I am with some of my blood relatives.

"Okay, we're good. Have a seat, it's going to be interesting," He says and we sit at his business desk facing each other. "It's like this...Yes, I entered into this arranged marriage idea," He does the air quotations with his hands. "But I've had dreams about a woman who I cannot see her face. She is haunting me, torturing me and my Drake. I think she is my mate." Sighing, he starts to pace the room.

"That is deep, Draven. How long have you been dreaming of her?" I ask extremely curious.

"Since I matured." He looks distraught and I can't help but feel a little pity for him. "It's not that I don't trust you, Ladon." He looks at me as if he's pleading for understanding. "It's that I wasn't sure that it meant she was my mate, but now I'm positive it's her, she's meant to be mine" he says with conviction in his voice.

I lean back and stroke my short beard pondering the ramifications of what Draven just told me. "Can you describe her to me? Or can you show me?" Raising my right brow curiously I expose a family secret. "My mother, sister and I can share visions and memories. I can probably probe your memories, but I'd need my mom to walk me through how to do it right." I tilt my head to the side waiting for Draven's thoughts on the matter.

"We should be able to. I mean, my mom can so why can't I?" Draven says.

I walk over and lay my hands on his temples, close my eyes trying to find his astral plane. I figure since he's also a dragon it should exist. My dragon guides me to where Draven and his dragon is.

"This is the astral plane, it's a place for dragons and dragon-kin to go." I spread my arms wide and spin slowly. "My family and I use it to communicate over great distances or anytime we are separated." I walk over and lay my hands on my dragon's scales. "Even though we are one, here he can do as he pleases and speaks to the other animals in the family. Usually, he and Tia's dragoness curl up like they did when they were hatchlings." I smile looking at my friend. "I want you to think back, remember your dream, take me there with you," I say, walking forward and extending my hand to Draven.

Hesitantly he takes it and closes his eyes. The scenery around us slowly changes to the dreamscape. I know this land, it's near Appletree Hill. The flowers move like waves upon the ocean, the lush green grass sways constantly over the rolling hills. In the distance a maiden with long pale blonde hair that's curly at the end. Her dress is made of gossamer and is a pastel shade of pink. I watch her run towards the forest giggling, the ground turns to frost where her bare feet touch.

She turns just enough to give me her side profile, and I'm ninety percent sure I know who it is. I look down at my right wrist and move the leather band I have there. I bear

*the same birthmark, the twin crescent moons. Part of me
wants to cry tears of joy for both my friend and the maiden
in question. I think I'm going to surprise my friend and
extend an invitation to Tia to watch the tournament. That
way I can introduce them afterward and I can see if I'm
right or not.*

I pull us out of Draven's dream and back into reality.
Draven looks at me hoping I have the answer to his problem. "So? Do you know her? Please, tell me you do." I've
never seen Draven look so desperate.

I need to phrase this properly so he doesn't get his hopes
up if I'm wrong. "She has ice as I do, and there are very
few families that have daughters." I shrug my shoulders
trying to appear as relaxed as possible.

"I'll see what I can figure out for you. For now, I need to
go make phone calls. I'll meet you in the dining room in a
little bit." I say to Draven as I grab my clothes and head
into the bathroom. I listen to him leave the room and
close the door behind him. I've got my work cut out
for me.

~Draven~

I CAN TELL Ladon is hiding the truth from me as to
who the woman is. The one detail I left out is the crescent moon tattoo on her wrist. I've never seen anything
like it. It looks more like a birthmark, almost too faint to

see but I see it every night. Not to mention he smelled like *her* or she is here somewhere nearby. I can almost pull the scent of rain from my memory from today and bathe in the smell.

"Hello, Draven." Cringing I turn slowly and see the one female I wish I could avoid walking towards me.

Damn it, not now. "Greetings Raven. How are you this evening?" I ask politely trying to remain as neutral as possible. She makes my skin crawl thinking about how she's slept her way through most of the squad trying to find a suitable mate.

"I would have been better had we been spending time together today. What have you been up to?" She purrs at me. This horrid female has been chasing me for years. Her family isn't exactly honorable. Underneath it all she wishes to be my mate to gain control of the throne.

"As you heard earlier, Ladon arrived and we have been catching up. What have you been doing?" I ask through gritted teeth. Having to be polite because of my station, royally sucks at times like this.

"Oh you know, what women do best." Raven says as she trails her fingers between her breasts. Her hand slowly slips lower heading to her lower stomach before I turn my head away from her.

"You mean what you do best. Sleeping around again from the smell of it," I accuse, she reeks of sex and from what I can tell it was more than one male.

"I'm shocked, Draven," she says stepping back from me. "You're the only one I want to be with but you aren't even doing *that* duty well," she spits out.

"Hell itself would freeze over first, besides your needs are not my duty to attend to." I say mockingly, "I won't touch you with a ten-foot pole and you know it. You are only after me for power and you deserve nothing more than to run amuck in a brothel," I say angrily, my eyes narrow as I feel my Drake flare to the surface..

Raven turns with her back to me and her shoulders are tight. "You're a bastard, Draven."

"Really? Is that the best you've got? Retract your statement before I make a mage stop your resurrection." I say, raising my voice. Raven's tune changes almost instantly and the scent of fear fills the air with an acrid scent.

"I'm sorry, dearest, my tongue got away with me. What I meant was...you need to wake up and take me as your mate." She smiles sweetly. "A phoenix can only strengthen your bloodline." She blows a kiss at me then walks away.

The gaul of that girl is infuriating, how dare she! I pray I can find my true mate to get rid of this girl. I really just want to pick her up in my talons and slice her to pieces across her family's yard. She is the most rotten, spoiled bitch I've ever met and I've met many women looking for my mate. A few minutes pass by as I stand there trying to remain calm. Suddenly, I feel a hand clasp over my shoulder, startling me.

"What's wrong, D?" Ladon asks as I turn to face him.

"Firstly, you're damn light on your feet. Second, do you have any idea how hard it is to be an enforcer and *not* kill someone you hate?" I ask, still fuming. My eyes shift to that of my dragon and glow an eerie green.

"I bet, my mom says that all the time about the one advisor," Ladon says with a smirk and a chuckle. "As for the light on the feet thing, have you ever lived in a house full of Wolves? I swear I think they can hear a mouse fart in the woods." Ladon chuckles then begins to pace the room.

"That female smells like she's bedded half the defense teams. What the fuck dude?" Ladon throws his hands up in the air. "Do your parents know she's this much of a tramp?" Ladon says exasperated.

"Sadly, no. They think she's the greatest thing that graced our kingdom," I say in disgust. "She stays away from my family for the most part. I'm lucky that my parents are giving me an out or I really might start a war on my own by killing her," I say with a twisted smile because that thought makes me incredibly happy.

Ladon smirks at me, nodding his head in agreement. "You are my brother for sure and I'll have your back. If you don't kill her first, I might." The way Ladon smiles almost concerns me. "Now let's go eat, I'm starving after my flight."

I smile at him, punching him in the gut. "You would eat an ox if anyone let you."

"Who says I haven't?" Ladon shrugs feigning innocence.

We laugh and rough house as we head to the dining hall. The guards are smiling at our playfulness as it's something they haven't seen from me often. We practically tumble into the room and almost knock over my Aunt's Lea and Aspen. "So sorry! I wasn't watching where we were going!"

"Draven, I am glad to see you are in great spirits and have your number one comrade at your side," Aspen says beaming at me.

"I am lucky Ladon is here," I say, punching him in the shoulder. He smiles and greets my aunts.

"Welcome, Ladon. We hope you enjoy your stay and the tournament," says Aunt Lea.

"I will do so, thank you," Ladon says politely with a small bow.

"See you later aunties, we are starving!" I give them quick pecks on the cheeks and take off with Ladon.

"Your aunts are quite the pair." Ladon says as he tries not to laugh.

"If you mean trouble, then yes they are." I tell him. We find our places and are served quickly by the staff. Our plates are full with tomahawk steaks, mushroom risotto, petite golden potatoes, and green beans with bacon. We don't speak until our entire meal is consumed along with our mugs of dark beer. Ladon leans back rubbing his stomach and chest expressing how full he is.

"That...was a delicious meal, brother. That was a meal fit for a king!" Ladon stretches out and his back pops in several places. His phone dings several times in rapid succession.

Quickly he pulls it out of his pocket and his eyes fly over the messages. "Tia says my parents are inbound and should arrive within the hour. Can you alert the guard to their arrival while I go speak with Tia?" I look up at him briefly.

"She always stresses when everyone leaves her," Ladon says with a genuine smile, he worries about his sister and it warms my heart to see how close they are.

"I'll go find them and we will catch up in an hour in your room," I tell him with a forcing smile.

Ladon rolls his eyes and says, "Yes, please."

We get up from our table, clasp hands like guys do and go our separate ways. Now to see how my family reacts when they hear Ladon's parents have accepted their invitation to the tournament.

THREE

LADON

As soon as Draven is out of sight I haul ass back to my room. I can only hope I'm right and my sister won't feel so alone all the time. Quickly, I lay down a layer of ice on the door and surrounding floor to prevent intruders from sneaking up on me. I move around the room securing all of the windows. I double-check the door and my ice layer before I go to get comfortable.

I move to sit in the center of my bed with my legs crossed. My hands are cupped, with my palms facing up, as I close my eyes to find my center. My breathing slows to the point I can clearly hear my heartbeat and settle deeply into the astral plane. *"Tia,"* I call out to my sister knowing full well she will appear almost as soon as I call for her. Gently I pull on her essence so that she arrives quickly and knows it's important.

Within seconds Tia and her dragoness come running towards us. Her dragoness and my dragon curl up together while Tia and I embrace. "Sissy? I have a rather odd ques-

tion for you, about your dreams." I smile looking down at my sister before I kiss her temple.

Tia immediately gets fidgety and pulls away from me. "Why, whatever do you mean?" She looks nervous, I'm definitely onto something. "Um...," She begins to pace and then looks back at me. Her eyes are that of her dragon and she's leaving a trail of frost two feet wide. This level of anxiety can only mean one thing, she's hiding something.

"Talk to me sissy, I can't fix it if you don't talk to me." I try to look as calm as possible, not giving away anything that I already suspect.

Tia lowers her eyes and sighs softly. "It's easier if I show you, brother." Tia's body radiates power as she begins to change the astral plane. I feel the flux of her power curl around me, as if a warm blanket is wrapping me up, as she starts changing the environment at her whim.

Moments like this she scares me, her mastery of the astral plane and frost rivals our mother's. The scene around us begins to change, it starts by Appletree Hill and then moves to Mirror Lake. In the lake is a broad-shouldered man with his back to us just wearing pants. It's definitely Draven, I was with him when he got that tribal tattoo. I smirk knowing, as usual, I was fucking right.

"Every night it's the same Ladon, he stands there in hip-deep water." Tia motions to the man in question. "He vexes me, his scent wraps around me and I swear I drag it back with me." She starts pacing, the trail of frost is getting wider by the minute.

"No matter where I move on the lakeshore I can't see his face!" Tia screams and ice and frost shoots out in every direction from her like a bomb detonating. The force of the impact from her power almost knocks me off my feet.

My sister is in pain to a level I would never have suspected from her. Hesitantly I walk over and wrap my arms around her. Gently I lay my cheek on the crown of her head keeping her tucked tightly against me. "Shh...I've got you, sissy. Come visit me as my guest at the tournament."

I pull back just enough to be able to make eye contact with her. "There are some really awesome people I want you to meet. Who knows? You may find Mr. Tall Dark and Brooding." I raise a eyebrow and smile at my sister trying to gauge her reaction

Tia smiles and nods her head. "Definitely, that would be nice." She finally smiles for real. "Mom and Dad are supposed to be there so at least I have them while you're busy. See you soon Ladon." Tia bounces up and kisses my cheek, then she's gone and I'm shoved back into my room.

I QUICKLY REMOVE the ice and get changed to be ready to go see my parents when they arrive... I double check my appearance then look to the door expecting Draven to arrive at any moment. Speaking of Draven, I hear him taking lazy steps. It might be that the conversation went well with his parents, or he'd be stepping a lot harder.

"Ladon, are you dressed?" Draven asks as he knocks. "I don't want to see you naked again. Remember how bad it was the last time?" he asks as he laughs.

I open the door unexpectedly and punch him in the gut. "Yeah, I remember, it was hilarious," I say with sarcasm obvious in my voice. Sharing a room when he came to visit once was not ideal as we both tend to go nude.

"So...What would you say if? "I raise my eyebrows at him. "I told you I think I found your mystery woman...," I smirk at him watching his expressions. "And she will be at the tournament?" I cross my arms over my broad chest watching Draven's expression with sadistic glee.

"I'm sorry...*what* did you just say?" He asks an octave higher than usual. His eyes widened in shock.

"Did I stutter?" I raise an eyebrow just watching his facial expressions change rapidly.

"I fucking knew it! You knew who it was all along, didn't you?" Draven exclaims practically jumping out of his skin. He throws his arms up in the air then back down to his side quickly.

I casually shrug my shoulders and start to laugh. "I had my suspicions. I didn't want to get your hopes up and be wrong." I soften my smile attempting to be sympathetic. "That would have sucked harder. Besides..." I smirk knowingly. "This female will more than likely decimate

Raven and any other suitor in a heartbeat and no one would dare raise a hand to her." I wink my eye at him knowing full well my sister will destroy her.

I punch Draven in the shoulder. "You better bring your A-game to the tournament." I get a little smug. "She's going to be watching." I know my sister the minute she catches his scent she will be on him like kids on candy. We have mom to thank for the heightened sense of smell, sometimes being part Lycan isn't such a bad thing.

"I would love to see her take down Raven! And you know I will give everything I've got and I'll win, just for her," Draven says with conviction in his voice and happiness shining in his eyes.

"She's already a big fan, man," I say confidently, smiling broadly. "Consider Raven dead, she just doesn't know it yet." I know the level of possession and loyalty the females in my family have, and you can bet your ass any threat to what's theirs will not live long.

"Though, if you really want to impress this particular female." I raise an eyebrow at him.

"I can have her favorite flowers waiting for her if you want? I can totally do you that solid." I smile excitedly to see my best friend, my brother truly happy.

"I would appreciate the help, Ladon, truly." Draven shakes his head at me. It's nice to see my best friend honestly looking hopeful. "I'm not shocked that you're still withholding her identity from me." He purses his lips for a moment before creasing his brows.

"Can I guess at least? I'm dying here, brother." It's clear his beast is waging war as his eyes keep shifting to that of his dragon.

"Hmmm...I guess it wouldn't hurt." I say as I tap my index finger on my chin. "Though being a dragon I like my treasure, and this is very valuable information." I chuckle softly, I'm enjoying this entirely too much.

"One guess, I haven't even told the lass I know whom the male she's been dreaming of is." I adjust the leather band over my right wrist making sure my birthmark is covered.

"You know I will treasure her like the rarest gem." I watch his flames and lightning flicker over his fingertips anxiously. "So if you'll give me only one guess...is it Jayce and your mother's child?" Draven asks curiously, knowing that Luna has white hair.

I bust out laughing, doubling over and almost dropping to my knees. "Hell no brother! Trust me, that's one girl you don't want." I shake my head no and raise my hands to punctuate my statement.

"She's an Omega through and through and would never survive the life we lead. Plus she's already betrothed." I say bluntly. I tap my chin several times. "I'll trade you a second guess." By the look on Draven's face I know I've piqued his interest.

"The lass in question loves knives, so if you give me one to present to her you can guess again." I tilt my head looking at Draven, I really am starting to understand my mother's sick enjoyment when it comes to torturing us with presents.

"You know I'll do anything for her, no matter the cost," Draven says passionately.

"She loves collecting small Damascus knives. Father has to have mother check her bodice to make sure she's not carrying any all the time." I smirk looking at Draven. Quickly Draven pulls out a knife he had made himself and offers it to me. "I'm sure she will love this token," I say as I look up at Draven. "You can take a second guess brother." I smile and wait patiently.

"The blade is folded Damascus steel in a ladder pattern. Several hundred folds ensure it is the strongest blade around." Draven smiles with pride as he motions to the blade. "Just like us Ladon, its strength comes from great effort. I hope to be allowed to put that same effort into a long relationship with my mate." Draven is truly wearing his heart on his sleeve.

"Don't look at me like that, I know I'm a lovesick fool, but how can I not be? Look at who my folks are." Draven scratches his cheeks, frustrated. "Dare I ask, is it...your twin?" He asks quietly, afraid of how I might react.

"Did you by chance see any identifying marks on the lass?" I slightly shrug my shoulders. "Just a quick question before I answer you honestly brother." He's hit the nail on the head. I just want to draw it out a bit more.

"Damn your games, Ladon!" He says then bows his head. Slowly he runs his hands through his long hair then looks up to me hopeful. "Yes, she has a mark. It's a crescent moon that is barely visible on her right wrist." Draven absently rubs the spot on his wrist where mine and Tia's birthmarks are.

"I missed it for a long time before I finally paid more attention." Draven looks up to me hopeful that I will answer him this time. "Now tell me, please, this is the worst torture imaginable and trust me—I'll repay you when your time comes." Draven implores.

"I bet you will, my friend...I bet you will." I smile and shift a finger on my left hand to my talon and cut the leather ties that hold the band around my right wrist. I rub my birthmark, the twin crescent moons before I show Draven my wrist. "Tia and I have the same birthmark."

SHOCK IS evident across Draven's face as he stares at me in disbelief. If he wasn't such a good friend I would be laughing like a hyena but these two are dear to me and I dare not laugh. I am thrilled he finally knows, though working him up was fun.

"You're...not yanking my wing, are you?" He says as I watch the tears starting to well up in his eyes. "Please, Ladon, say this is not one of your pranks," Draven says choked up. He reaches forward and grips my forearm staring at my birthmark.

"No prank, you've been haunting her dreams as well." I smile happily to reveal Tia's biggest secret.

"Look into my memories, see what she showed me today. Look at yourself from her perspective." I offer my hands to my brother, I'll do anything to help soothe him and reassure him that his happy ever after is a reality.

Draven takes my hands and probes my mind seeing himself exactly how Tia perceives him. After a few moments, he pulls away with his eyes still closed and tears leaking down in continuous streams.

"Tia is everything I could ever have dreamed of and more." He sighs softly. "I can't believe the way I appear to her." He shakes his head slowly. "She looks at me, like how I feel about her right now. That she's a miracle made flesh." Draven says wistfully.

I pull Draven in for a brief bro-hug then I back up. "If it was anyone other than you I would probably haunt that mother fucker making sure he treats my sister right." I back away and look out the window of my bedroom. "She should be arriving by tonight sometime. I'll keep watch for her and bring her to my room so she's comfortable."

"But then again.." I pause reconsidering my plan of action. "Maybe having her this close to you could cause the premature murdering of half the females here. We don't want you executed when you're this close to getting your true mate." I give a definitive nod.

"I'll have a room made up for her in one of the other wings and I'll go stay with her there." I clap him on the back. "I'll make sure her favorite flowers fill her room waiting for her arrival." I smile trying to reassure Draven.

"I've got you, brother, no worries." We fist bump and share a good laugh. I remain with Draven until he gets his emotions under control.

"LET'S go catch up with your parents, mine should be arriving at any moment." We leave my room quickly, Draven's mood has vastly improved since this morning. "They are thrilled to have your parents coming. My father is more so than mom but that's because he loves Alaric like a brother, as I do you," Draven tells me. "I guess the apple didn't fall far from the tree!"

"Speak for yourself! I don't partake in male pleasure, only females for me," I say matter of factly.

"Well, me either! You know what I meant." Draven hits my shoulder, "we are here."

The door to the royal chambers is made of carved wood. The intricate patterns show a pair of dragons locked in battle. I am about to reply when I hear Gisella tell us to come in. Draven leads the way and I follow shortly behind him. "Hello, mom," he says and kisses her cheeks.

"Hello again, Draven," she says beaming at him. "Hello, Ladon! I've been told your parents should be arriving anytime now. I am pleased to see them once again. It's been a long time."

"Yes, your highness, it has been. I am sure they are ecstatic to see you two as well. Where is Austin?" I inquire.

"He is already getting ready for the tournament and for your father's arrival." Gisella rolls her eyes and smiles.

"No doubt those two will go at it trying to best each other," Gisella says giggling. "Let's all go down and get ready for their formal arrival."

WE ALL HEAD OUT and get ready for my parents imminent arrival. This should be interesting. We arrive on the grounds of the expansive castle. I mentally start preparing myself for the chaos that might occur when Tia arrives. I know I'll have to hold Draven back from rushing to her.

We find Draven's father at the blacksmiths table admiring a long sword that is beautifully crafted. There are many different tents around the ground as well as the tournament grounds. I feel as if I've stepped back into medieval times, it's perfect.

We all say our greetings before hearing the massive roar that is my mother and then my father. I can't wait for this to all unfold. I watch my father circle the castle grounds then he moves towards the tournament tents. He heads to the field nearby and lands gracefully. Mother slides off his back and digs his clothing out for him.

"Mom, Dad!" I run over and embrace my mother first then when Dad's dressed I hug him too.

"You seem overly jovial Ladon." Alaric raises an eyebrow looking at me, I know he suspects something is up.

"I'm with my brother-in-arms, and there's a massive tournament tomorrow." I draw in a deep breath and look at my mother and she gets the hint. She knows what I've done and it makes her smile.

"Ok, I know you two are up to something." Alaric narrows his eyes looking between my mother and I just as Draven and his parents catch up to us.

"*Alaric!*" Austin hollers running up and bear-hugging my father.

"Austin, it's been far too long! Thank you for inviting us!" Alaric says with a massive smile.

The only other person to make father smile that way is mom. I'll enjoy this for now because I know their attitudes will change later and not for the better.

"Aurora! Hello, darling. Thank you for gracing us for this occasion," Gisella says with a small courtesy to show my mother respect. That's always a smart choice.

"Gisella..." Aurora raises both eyebrows at her watching her courtesy to her. She still hasn't adjusted to court life after all these years. She would rather fight than attend royal functions.

"It is so nice to see both of you! Thank you for inviting us!" Aurora moves in briefly to embrace Gisella and nuzzle her cheek before backing up. "We should arrange visits more often."

"Mother...," I warn her, looking to Draven who is looking curiously at me.

"We should all get ready for the feast tonight. Draven can show you to the royal guest wing," Austin says.

WE ALL MAKE our way back inside to spruce up for the night. What an eventful one it shall be. Draven takes us to another wing and asks a servant to fetch my things. We part ways quickly, get showered and changed into formal attire.

Mother is particularly quiet and father keeps shooting her looks. He doesn't like being on the outside of inside knowledge. Before we leave the room he perks up and is in a different mindset from the looks of it, they must have talked through the mate bond telepathically.

I smirk knowingly as we begin walking towards the dining hall. Walking into the room is always breathtaking as it's decorated immaculately with large rustic wooden round tables, floral decor, and of course silver dinnerware and goblets.

We take our seats where the card tents have us listed and wait for Draven and his family. We don't have to wait long before they join us and it's a good thing because I'm starving again. Alaric and Austin sit next to each other as do Draven and I, leaving the women in the middle.

Servers come by taking our orders and filling our goblets with rich red wine. Conversations begin breaking out as Gisella's Aunts', Lea and Aspen arrive.

"Draven, we saw the most curious thing a few minutes ago before we came in." Aspen tilts her head to the side. "Raven is circling the castle outside as if she's watching for something. Why would she be acting so strangely?" Aspen inquires.

"She never flies at night and certainly not by herself," Draven says frustrated. "She's probably trying to get my attention," he mutters standing up and heading outside before dinner even starts.

Mother sits back watching everything going on, something isn't sitting right with her. Dad notices the scales rippling behind Mom's ear as she looks in the direction that Draven went. "Ladon go check on your brother...Something isn't right." Mom leans into Dad's side trying to calm herself. I leave the table as soon as mother suggests it.

An ethereal glow fills mom's eyes just before her head whips towards the door. Tia is coming in hot, that girl is super excited and in a rush to arrive. Tia's roar can be heard clear as day. Everyone makes their way outside quickly to wait for her.

FOUR

TIAMAT

Today is the best day of my entire existence. My beloved little brother has found my mate. I can't wait to see them both. I pack a single bag with my favorite dresses and one pair of evil shoes.

I had to freeze Dante and Edgar to their chairs to escape without an escort, a girl has to do what a girl has to do. Quickly I strip and take flight, remembering to grab my bag before I left.

The winds are in my favor making the trip that much easier and faster. I ride the thermals catching a break with a strong southern wind. The miles seem to melt by as I cross land and now the ocean.

I start to get hungry because I am not used to flying for this length of time. I dive down briefly into the ocean and eat a dolphin to keep up my strength for the remainder of the flight. With a full stomach I continue my journey, now crossing over the mainland of the island.

The island itself is the most beautiful place I've ever seen. There's so many different plants and scents it's impressive. I can't wait to see this place in the daylight instead of at dusk.

My heart starts pounding in my chest when I see the castle in the distance. I roar, calling out to my family and mate. A plume of frost escapes with my roar and I happily fly through it. I'm so close to my forever I can almost taste it.

The scent of sandalwood drifts up to me and I roar again. I do a barrel roll, I'm so excited. *He's here, he's really here.. My mate... I can smell him and I'm awake, just a little further.* I flap my wings furiously trying to close the distance even faster.

A SCREECHING call breaks me out of my inner monologue, I look to my right and a ball of fire is barreling towards me. I contemplate evasive maneuvers, but the bloody thing is so much smaller than me. *What the hell is that thing?* I say to myself. The flaming asshole shoots a funnel of fire directly at me with full intention of killing me. Screw that! I bank to the right, taking the flames to my underbelly.

Oh hell no! My snow-white fur is burned off of my scales, now that pisses me off. This ball of screeching fire has no clue who it messed with!

The firebird starts to look like it's confused and almost panicked. It calls for backup and a small brown dragon joins it. They both attempt to attack me with their breath weapons. I guess the firebird wasn't expecting its fire not to work. This dumb flaming fire turd has positioned itself between me and the castle.

The brown dragon comes in hard and fast. Without hesitation I breathe my permafrost breath weapon on it. The dragon didn't stand a chance. It plummets like a ton of bricks and shattered upon the lawn. The firebird is still blocking my path, and that was the birds final fatal mistake. Is it trying to stop me from getting to my mate? *Not today Satan, not today...*

I immediately go on the offensive and start to chase the firebird down. Every beat of my wings I feel my blood boiling. Stupid fire turd trying to stop me from getting to my mate. In my mind I hear my mother telling me to end it and stop playing with my food.

My ignitor clicks and I start spewing my permafrost breath weapon again. The flaming bird screeches in fear seeing the blast of permafrost just barely missing it. It's so much colder than my frost flames and if anything it will freeze this asshole solid, fire or not.

The firebird narrowly avoids the first shot, but not the second. I freeze that flaming asshole solid and watch the ice ball as it falls to the ground. It also shatters upon impact. Just before I'm able to dive and go after it again my father comes at me fast, and leads me off towards the other side of the castle. I hope my bag is intact in my taloned hand, otherwise this could be quite embarrassing.

Draven

I CAN SMELL the rain scent getting stronger as if a storm is on the horizon. I tail Ladon as we race to get outside not wanting to miss a thing. I watch anxiously as the aerial battle ensues. The silver-white dragon dwarfs the two attackers. It fires a breath weapon I've never seen before lighting up the sky.

The brown dragon plummets and shatters into a hundred pieces. Raven's phoenix is on the run from the dragon I can only assume is my mate. The first blast of the breath weapon misses, but the second strikes true and Raven's frozen form plummets to the ground. Upon impact it shatters as well, there's no resurrection after that.

Alaric has already taken off from the looks of it. I take my eyes off of Tia for a moment and now she's gone. I guess her father collected her to bring her to their room. Raven's head is in a solid block of ice, frozen mid-screech. It takes everything in me not to laugh but I wind up snorting instead.

Her best friend Janel is in at least a hundred frozen chunks across the yard. That woman of mine really packs a punch or in her case--throws some wicked ice. I take off to look for Tia, she couldn't have gone far. I should be a gentleman and allow her to change after her shift. I remember their family doesn't keep their clothes intact like ours does.

Ladon approaches me with a slight hesitancy, which is completely unlike him. "Brother, are you okay?" Ladon asks.

"I am holding it together although every fiber of my being says to go to her, now," I tell him quietly. "I don't know how I will be able to wait until the official mating ceremony, Ladon." Ladon furrows his brows looking at me.

"That's intense, Draven. What's a mating ceremony?" Ladon asks puzzled.

"Well, my mother's people tend to not touch intimately till we are married." Draven shrugs his shoulders.

"Ah, that makes sense." Ladon sighs and looks somber. "What I do know is that it's Tia's first kills and our father will need to be there for her. We can see her at dinner if they choose to come down." He glances back towards where his parents room is.

"After a long flight, I am sure Tia would have an appetite to some degree," Ladon says softly.

"You're right, thank you, Ladon. Though I don't think wine will be my choice of drink tonight. It's time for the aged bourbon," I say rubbing the spot over my chest, my heart is thumping out of my ribcage.

"Let's fly right quick and loosen up before we hit the bottle," Ladon suggests. I nod in agreement and hit him with some temporary magic to seal his clothes to his shift. We walk a few yards away from the crowd and take off.

Fuck them all, I'm so tired of everyone believing I am such a saint. My love for my friends, family and my woman might be overly affectionate but to anyone else--if you cross me, I will end you.

I blow out some fire and play in it trying to relax until Ladon hits me in the foot with some ice, dragging me down a little, asshat. We play around for a while taking jabs at each other as I search the ground for Tia. I get a little sidetracked now and again looking for her anywhere on the premises before we land.

"Thanks for the clothing assist. I would hate to have had all the damsels here fawning all over me in all my naked glory," Ladon says laughing.

"Yeah, I've seen the naked glory...it's not all it's cracked up to be," I jab at him.

"You're a dick." Ladon says jokingly.

"Have one, not one," I say smiling at him like an idiot. Ladon only rolls his eyes at me as we walk in silence back to the dining hall.

ALARIC MAKES his way back into the dining area. The fresh scent of rain carries on the wind grabbing my attention. Tia is walking directly behind Alaric holding her father's hand with her head hung low.

The pale pink gossamer dress from my dreams catches in the wind giving a hint to her form. My eyes drift up towards her angelic face, tears are rolling freely down her cheeks. I can tell the guilt of taking a life is weighing heavily on her heart. Ladon is starting to rub his sternum, feeling his sister's pain and anguish.

Tia slowly steps forward away from her father and holds her wrists out in Austin's direction. "Please forgive my trespass." She draws in a deep breath. "I didn't mean to kill two of your people. Do with me what you will." Tia's voice is shaky as she speaks. She's fully submitting to my father and the crown awaiting punishment. The ground beneath her bare feet is steadily freezing solid. She refuses to look up at anyone, she must be feeling she has failed her parents. Her long pale blonde curls fall to cover her face from my view.

"Tia no!" Ladon yells at her, then starts to move towards his sister. Alaric raises a single hand stopping his son in his tracks.

Tia slowly shakes her head no, she drops to her knees awaiting her sentencing. She folds her hands submissively in her lap with her head hung low.

"Tia, dear, you are not in trouble. You were invited along with your parents, therefore, you have done nothing wrong, but on another note..." He helps her up with one hand delicately, and I begin a deep growl, "You were fighting for love and your mate. That can never be held against you," he finishes and releases her hand and I stop threatening my own blood.

Tia looks up to Austin with her pale grey-blue eyes and smiles softly at him. I watch her tilt her head when I growled at my father.

"Are you sure, sir? I killed a flaming bird and a brown dragoness." She raises her delicate eyebrows questioningly. "I've never seen a flaming bird before. It burnt my fur off my belly, I really wasn't happy." Tia still sounds like she doesn't believe she's not in trouble. "Father says never to strike out in anger and I did. It was blocking my path." Tia lowers her eyes further.

"You will never be in harm's way again in our kingdom," I tell her, unable to take my eyes off her stunning features.

I hear Tia finally release the breath she didn't realize she was holding, having heard my voice so close to her. Gently she wipes her eyes and looks from Austin to me. She draws in a sharp breath, shock written across her face, finally being able to see me in the flesh. Frost lightly coats her skin as well as her long pale blonde hair. A blush creeps over her cheeks before she looks down again. "Thank you...I...Appreciate it." She bites her bottom lip looking frustrated that she might sound unsure of herself.

Goddess, she's adorable! Breathe man, breathe, and play it cool. Don't freak out.

"Let us all relax and enjoy dinner, shall we?" My mom asks, breaking the tension that is building between us and everyone staring.

Tia nods slowly and then runs over to her father and whispers in his ear. I'm quite curious as to what she's asking him. Alaric looks from me then to my father then back down to Tia. "I'm not sure baby girl." Alaric kisses his daughter's forehead and holds her to his chest.

I can hear a soft whine from Tia which prompts Aurora to take her daughter from her father. The resemblance is uncanny, it's as if Aurora cloned herself. I watch Tia whisper to her mother and Aurora's eyes shift to that of her beast as she examines my father and me. She looks back at her daughter and kisses her cheek. "Go ahead and ask your questions, little one, don't be afraid." Aurora scoots Tia away from her.

Tia almost looks panicked as she looks again from me to my father. Slowly she walks to stand before my father again. Her hands are fidgeting with the material of her dress. "I don't know if it's considered rude in your culture but may I inquire as to what beast my mate has?" She glances quickly in my direction then back to my father. "I sense his fire, I do not wish to insult your customs by speaking directly to him without your permission." Tia lowers her head being respectful of my father's station.

"I also wish to question if the scale exchange would be permitted since we are not required to touch each other intimately to do it." Her right hand comes up tentatively and touches her chest over her heart, I assume it's where the scale will be placed. "My brother can be my proxy and pass things between us." I can hear Tia sigh as she motions to Ladon. I can feel the anxiety coming off her in waves.

My heart is pounding out of my chest at her request and my ears are humming. The anticipation of being so close to her and yet so far away is plaguing my heart. Please let my father say yes!

"You are welcome to speak freely, my dear," my father states. "The scale exchange is an ancient custom. How does one so young have knowledge of it?" Austin questions.

Tia smiles broadly and motions to her parents. "My parents are true mates, they exchanged scales and the scales live." Tia bites her lower lip. "It's the only way to truly know if your son is my destined mate."

My father looks between Tia and me then over to my mom. Mom gives him a nod and he turns back to Tia. "I will allow the exchange via proxy." My father motions for us to proceed.

Our eyes lock and the tension is building. Tia has frost covering her feet and skin as I have fire in my clenched fists. Ladon moves to Tia first awaiting his sister's next move. Out of the corner of my eye I catch Aurora coming up along the side of her daughter with a silk bag. Tia nods to her mother and the bag is removed revealing a large snake-like skull with serrated teeth and heavy bone plates on its forehead.

Tia looks briefly up to me as she passes her treasure to her brother. Ladon's eyes go wide looking at the skull in his hands. Just by the way he's looking at it, I know it's a huge deal.

Tia draws in a deep breath and slowly shifts her left arm to a heavily armored gauntlet. Her talons are long and thick and silver in color, her scales are as white as snow and appear to be razor-sharp. She looks over her gauntlet trying to find a scale she likes. A smile creeps across her ruby red lips as her right hand now also shifts and she cuts a scale from her gauntlet near her thumb. Quickly she lowers her mouth to her wound and licks it, sealing it shut. Ever so carefully she places the scale reverently in the center of the skull.

"As a right of passage, we are sent to hunt the Tizheruk, it's a large sea serpent that hunts the waters in the Bering Sea. Only the strongest Ice Dragons can capture and kill one since, like us it's immune to ice." Tia choses now to raise her eyes and look directly into mine. "I gift to you, my mate, my greatest accomplishment as my father did with my mother." Ladon heads towards me and offers me the skull and scale.

I accept my mate's prized possession completely impressed that she was able to kill such a powerful creature. Lightly my fingers ghost over the skull before touching her scale. Her silver white scale is cold to the touch, similar in temperature to a block of ice.

My Aunt Aspen comes from down the hall and over to my side. In front of her she pushes a box that contains the skull from one of my more difficult kills. Carefully I pull the pins and the sides open. The skull within is a basilisk, one of the more deadly creatures to battle.

I shift my arms to my gauntlets, my scales are bronze and gold. Carefully I remove a scale near my thumb as well and place it upon the skull. Ladon carefully takes the skull and scale to Tia.

"Tia my love, my beast is a mix of Gold and Bronze dragons." I smile softly as I motion to the skull before her. "I hope you find it worthy," I say staring at her as Ladon presents the skull to her.

Tia's anxiety slowly disappears as her brother approaches her. "You already know what I am." She blushes a pretty rose color before accepting my offering from her brother. "It's beautiful thank you." She says before shifting her hand again.

In her left hand she's holding my scale, her right hand comes up quickly and she plunges her talon into her chest right above her heart. Tia quickly shifts her right hand back and takes my scale sticking the flesh side into the wound she created. A small rivulet of blood rolls down her chest.

I lunge forward before my father and her father steps in to stop me. I desperately want to heal her. My dragon is growling at the sight of her blood although our father's strength around my chest tells me it will all be alright. So I wait and watch as the wound seals over my scale and is now a part of her chest.

Tia looks at me curiously with a small smile and her head tilted. Our fathers' release me, moving aside, waiting for me to do my part. I take her scale in my left hand as I shift my right and dig my talon into my chest over my heart. Quickly I sink the flesh side of her scale into my wound. As it heals I feel a small chill then warmth surrounding my heart which tells me it was accepted. I'm overcome with a sense of happiness that is not my own. I look at her and quirk an eyebrow and look at her wondering if it's her I am feeling.

Tia smiles softly and nods at me. "I feel you too." A single tear of joy slowly rolls down her cheek. Without thinking she attempts to close the distance between us, but fucking Ladon stops her. So much for being my brother-in-arms; I just got cock-blocked by my best friend.

I watch Tia bear her descended canines at her brother and start growling at him. It's not till Aurora comes up and gets in Tia's face does she settle down and remember where she is. Tia instantly changes her tune and appears sheepish and slightly embarrassed over how she acted. Her eyes dart between both sets of parents before she lowers her head. "Please forgive my inappropriate outburst. I forgot myself and almost broke protocol."

Aurora smirks and smacks Tia playfully on her ass. "I can't blame you little one, I would have done the same thing if your father was before me." She kisses Tia's temple before walking back to Alaric.

"Sorry if I hurt you Ladon. I forgot myself." Tia kisses Ladon's cheek then rests her head on his chest watching me.

"You didn't hurt me, Tia, and even if you did it would have been forgiven," Ladon tells her affectionately as siblings do.

"Let's feast! We have so much to celebrate!" exclaims Alaric.

Everyone moves on to sit at the tables in the hall but I can't unglue my feet as I stare at Tia in her pastel pink dress. Her chin is tilted down slightly and her hair drapes over her shoulder, allowing my scale to be seen by all to see. Pride makes my chest swell and the sight of her is pulling at my groin and I know I have to keep it in check or everyone will smell me. That would be embarrassing beyond all belief.

Tia keeps stealing glances in my direction, she is so shy and blushes every time I catch her. I really need to question Ladon as to what his sister does and doesn't know. Lucky for me Ladon and I are at the far end of the royal table with Tia and her parents at the other side.

"This is a rather awkward question man, but, why do I get the impression that Tia hasn't dated?" I whisper my question and watch Ladon's face grow pale.

"Dad raised her very old school just like my sister Kirra. They have never seen a male shift, nor anything below the beltline." Ladon's dragon's eyes flare for a second. "Do not hurt my sister, she's an innocent."

Bloody hell I think my heart just fell into the pit of my stomach. She personifies the title of a virgin bride. I will treat her with the utmost tenderness and bring her breakfast every morning. Ladon has no idea what lengths I will go to for his sister. "I swear, I won't. If anything she would hurt me. Don't repeat that to anyone. Swear it," I tell him through gritted teeth.

"You have my word. I must say though, you're smitten and it suits you," he says with a snicker as he kicks me.

"Ass... just wait... your time will come," I say under my breath. We all become immersed in conversation, drink, and food. As Tia tells Ladon about her trip I listen intently while taking a long pull of my beer and find it warm. What the hell? "Well, damn," I say softly and put my mug down with dissatisfaction.

Tia looks at the face I made after drinking my beer and smiles. Gently she touches my scale and gets my attention. She waves her drink at me then motions to mine. I make a yuck face and she giggles. I watch her eyes take on a white-blue glow around them and I watch my mug frost over before my eyes.

Ladon just shakes his head at his sister. "Show off!"

Tia gets a mischievous look in her eyes and her eyes glow again and then Ladon curses that his beer is frozen solid. Tia sticks her little pink tongue out at her brother and snuggles up with her father for the remainder of the evening.

LATER - THAT NIGHT-

I make Tia a massive bubble bath with tons of bubbles and a lilac bath bomb my mom gave me. She said it would help her relax before bed tonight. I'm just about to leave my note for her on the bathroom counter when she comes in with a white robe on. I was hoping to be out of here by now but now I'm glad I haven't left. "I am sorry, my love, I meant to be gone and it all would've been a surprise for you," I say, watching her cheeks glow pink.

"I am quite thankful, beloved, it's very thoughtful of you," Tia says softly, staring at me. "I should get ready for tomorrow."

She excuses herself with a small dip of her knee in respect to me but that's not what I want.

"Tia..." she stops on the spot with her back to me. I stay a foot away and whisper to her. "I hope you are able to relax and think of me as you do." I blow a hot breath across her neck and watch as goosebumps rise across her creamy skin. Her dragon rumbles in response to my teasing and it pleases me tremendously. "See you in the morning, my love." I say in a whisper.

I swiftly exit the room and head back to mine in the other wing. I have to take care of business or I might combust. I also need to grab my body spray and fumigate my room. Goddess forbid Tia comes up here for any reason and she smells anything other than me. I don't want a territorial mess going down. I've heard of how Aurora can go unhinged and that thought alone is enough for me to never upset Tia.

FIVE

TIAMAT

Draven was so thoughtful in setting up the bath for me. It warms my heart to think my mate is so caring. I lay there floating in the lilac scented bath worrying about if he will have eaten well enough for his tournament tomorrow. After my bath, I dress only in my robe and sneak out of the castle. I get far enough out of sight, drop my robe, and shift. I will hunt for my mate, I want him strong for the event that will be happening tomorrow.

I scour the hillsides and find a herd of red stag. Perfect. I find the largest buck and swoop down and kill it instantly. My sharp teeth rip through its neck ending its life. This should please my mate, he is a dragon after all. I pick up the stag in my talons and fly back towards the castle. I reach out through our fragile bond to find which side of the castle his room is on.

Thankfully Draven has a rather large balcony that I can deposit my present for him. I grip the rail with my dragon's taloned hands and shift back to my human form and pull myself over the rail. I use the blood of the stag to leave a note on the white marble of the patio.

Dear Beloved,

I couldn't sleep worrying about if you ate well or not. Please enjoy my gift, allow it to give you the strength you need to win tomorrow.

With love,
Tia

HESITANTLY I POKE my head into my mate's room and look around. I see him lying on the bed, the sheet barely over his hips. This is the most I've ever seen of a male. Almost all of his rippling muscles are on full display. I can't help but stare begging the Gods to make the sheet fall lower, my curiosity is definitely getting the better of me.

I'm half tempted to use my control of the arctic winds to move the sheet. I raise my hand tentatively and try to move the sheet without waking him. It inches down his stomach further till I can see the start of hair. He turns to his side and is facing me, thankfully his eyes are still closed. I can see the outline of something long and hard pressing against the sheet. My curiosity be damned, I must not stay any longer, my father would never forgive me if he found out I looked into Draven's room.

I reach up into my hair and cut a single braid free and lay it on my kill. Hopefully he will smell it and see what I had done for him. I leap off the balcony and shift back into my dragoness and fly swiftly off to my room, hopefully undiscovered. I get back to my wing of the castle and shift quickly and throw my robe on.

"What are you doing, sister?" Ladon asks, already knowing the answer.

I almost come unhinged...it's only Ladon, thank the gods. "You're one to speak," I say, trying to hide my blush.

"Don't change the subject. Why do I smell stag blood? You didn't do what I think you did, did you?" Ladon says suspiciously.

"Whatever do you mean, dear brother?" I ask him as I turn my head to hide my facial expression.

"You pulled a mom, I feel it in my gut," Ladon says accusingly then laughs. "Draven will have a nice wake up call indeed. Also, I am here not only to give you a hard time but to be your guardian so you don't try anything before your ceremony."

"I appreciate your concern, Ladon." I turn and face him head on. "Mom put you up to it though, did she not?" I prompt.

"Indeed she did. She knows you well and figured you might try something, and you did. It was a cute gesture, Tia." Ladon smiles looking at me.

"Thanks," I say blushing. "Now I need to sleep. Off with you now." Ladon nods and leaves the room to keep watch over me tonight. I might actually need him. The pull to be with Draven is strong as our bond grows. I crawl into bed with a silk nightgown on and fall asleep thinking of what Draven's Dragon will do when he sees my gift.

Draven

I WAKE up only to stretch and feel refreshed. For the first time since I was eight, I had a dreamless sleep. Was yesterday a dream? Did I really find my woman, and it's Tia? I sling my legs over the bed and rub my face. It's then I realize my balcony doors are open with the breeze bringing the smell of blood to my nose. I did not leave them open last night.

I throw on my grey sweatpants and head out to see what's going on. I don't have to walk far as there is a massive stag before me with a note and a pale blonde braid. Its neck has large puncture wounds for the kill and I have only one guess...Tia.

I read her note as I rub my chest where her scale lies. I think this is what humans' call butterflies. I take a picture of the note and grab the braid and leave it on my desk and head back outside. Quickly I throw my gift into the gardens below. I jump over the rail and shift roaring my thanks to my mate. The stag tastes divine and fills me. I shift back and head up to my room again.

I grab Tia's braid and smell it, calming my Drake. Thank the Goddess she left it or I might go burning the whole castle down to find her. Keeping our distance is far harder than I ever imagined, it's almost a worse torture than the years I spent dreaming about her. I put the braid down reluctantly and get ready for my day. Today, I will show her how strong I am by winning the entire tournament just for her. But first...I need a cold shower.

I dress in a dark grey tee and fitting jeans with black boots. I get to the balcony, ready to take flight once again. Echoing roars fill the air and it sounds like a battle is raging not far from the castle. It's then I see exactly what's going on. Up until now, I didn't realize how much larger Tia was than Alaric or even Ladon.

Next thing I know Tia's mom Aurora is standing next to me staring up at the mini-battle overhead. "Damn girl is way too much like me. Stubborn as all fucking hell and stronger than the men in the family." Aurora grumbles watching Tia making every attempt at heading towards my balcony. Thankfully her father and brother are immune to her frost otherwise there would be dragon-cicles on the palace grounds. They take turns blocking her every maneuver like a well choreographed dance in the air.

"Don't mind me being here Draven, I'm the last line of defense against my daughter. The ceremony is in less than forty eight hours and she *will* remain pure till then." Aurora looks at me and her eyes are that of her beast. It's quite concerning that this is my future mother-in-law, and wait, did she say pure?

"I'm sensing an underlying tone, your majesty. Do you mean to tell me she is a virgin?" I ask looking forward, avoiding eye contact with her.

"In every sense of the fucking word, Draven," Aurora says matter of factly.

Fuck my life...she's perfect. I need another cold shower now. I also feel guilty for teasing her the way I did when I got her bath ready for her. That was cruel and unusual punishment. I want desperately to go to her as she battles the men but I fight myself for control. I know if I do Aurora would take me down to protect her innocent daughter.

Aurora takes off and shifts as she launches off the balcony. She manages to freeze my feet to the balcony making me immobile. The aerial battle comes to an abrupt end as Alaric and Ladon drive Tiamat back to her side of the castle. I guess it's a huge help that her mother is doing some weird roar-howl thing at her as she chases after her daughter.

A few moments later my feet are free but wet. I warm them up and take off for breakfast. I will eat some though, even though I am not hungry after my loves treat.

I catch Ladon at the bottom of the stairs and we walk in silence to a table in the hall. We order quickly wanting to get to the ground for the tournament. "What's eating you, brother?" I ask Ladon.

"I'm aggravated...Tia is not her normal sweet self. Her dragoness is driving her to be with you and it's not easy to contain her." He throws his hands up in the air exasperated. "You saw her. She's larger than all of us and if she really wanted to she could put us all on our backs! The only one who can get her to see reason right now is mother," he says with a large exhale.

"I can see where you are coming from. Do you feel better now, getting that off your chest?" I ask as the servants bring us our meals.

"Yes, much, but killing something right now might be a better option. Actually...." he leans in closer to me, "where can I find a good place to blow off some frost?"

"There is always the Danae Macabre." I whisper, wiggling my eyebrows at him.

"You're the man!" He says clasping my hand then begins his meal.

I look around for Tia but I have a feeling in my gut that she won't be joining me this morning. Her mother probably has her locked down in a chastity belt.

TIA ENTERS the dining room slowly, her brows furrow and her eyes are locked on her brother. I almost didn't notice the beautiful floor-length blood-red gown. I said almost, if it wasn't for the fact that the dining room was suddenly feeling like we've been plunged into winter I'd be excited to see my mate. Something has royally set her off and I believe it's something Ladon has done.

"You told mother!" She shrieked at him as ice begins to form around his chair trapping him in his seat.

I'm thankful she didn't catch the earlier part of the conversation because I think I'd be a dead man by association. "Tia? Mother told me to keep an eye on you and to report to her what you've done. She would cut my balls off if I didn't tell her." Ladon says, trying to gain sympathy from his sister.

"You told on me! Shall I tell mother about where you're planning to go, brother dearest?" Tia tilts her head to the side, her eyes churning liquid mercury around her black dragon slits. She bares her canines at her brother as tiny scales ripple over her cheeks.

"As for you!" Her gaze suddenly whips over to me, I can feel in my chest the pain and anger and pain that is bubbling under the surface. "Don't...," she says shaking her head and I feel the fight drain out of her as she stares into my eyes, "just don't." A single tear rolls down her cheek and freezes there.

She moves to a seat at the far end of our table and waits for the staff to pull out the chair for her. She lowers herself into her seat and folds her hands in her lap. I watch her lower her head and refuse to meet my gaze.

My scale is visible on her chest and it appears to be pulsing in time with her heartbeat. If that's accurate, her heart is pounding a mile a minute like a hummingbird.

Her hand slowly raises and gently rubs my scale and it feels as though she's touching my chest. I stare at her scale in wonder. Does it work in both directions?

I pretend to take a bite of food and reach for her scale on my chest. I touch it as if I were caressing her hand letting her know that I am here, that I am not going anywhere. I wait for a facial response, but she is literally being an ice queen. Though I feel it differently through this bond we are creating. Tingles erupt over my hand, and creep up my arm, making me shiver. This must be how she feels.

"So, Tia," Ladon begins, "What did you do after your little impromptu flight last night?" He smirks after speaking.

I swear if I were drinking I would have spit it out. Tia snaps her head up and blushes a deep red that almost matches her dress. It's adorable but I am sure she wants to kill him right about now from the embarrassment I feel from her. Frost begins to coat Ladon's plate accompanied with a growl. "Ladon, behave," she says looking at the ice forming in front of her eyes. Aurora pops up with Alaric and my parents. Looks like things are about to get interesting.

"Ladon what did you do to set your sister off? You know she's struggling right now." Aurora says as she moves to kiss the crown of Tia's head.

Ladon shakes his head and looks at me then back to his mother. "I'm sorry Tia, I shouldn't have been teasing you," Ladon says, trying to sound remorseful.

Tia narrows her eyes as she stares at her brother. "Fine..." The terse answer is concerning, I can immediately tell whose temper my mate got. It certainly wasn't her father's and I now know my life will never be boring.

"Time to get a move on it, the tournament starts in one hour," my father says before digging into his plate.

I have to show Tia she's the only one for me. If only we could speak telepathically I could tell her how I feel without everyone's eyes on us and it being awkward. Frustration takes hold and it shows as I shove my seat back a little too hard and take off for the tents outside.

Before I get out of the room though I feel a small chill at my back and realize that it's Tia. I turn around and face her, staring at her stunning features. I watch as her pale grey-blue eyes swirl from dark to light and back again. It seems she is in as much turmoil as I am. I wonder...

"Tia." I say testing our tentative bond.

I see her eyes widen and her shoulders tense. *"Draven?"* She answers softly.

"Hello, my love. Are you alright?" I say gently.

"I will be once we are mated and have time alone. Not that I'm insinuating anything! I only wish to have time with you and not be under everyone's watchful eyes." Tia says nervously.

"I feel the same, Tia. I want to show you that I am worthy of you, that I'll protect you-always." I lightly rub her scale

trying to soothe her. *"I want to get this out now. I don't want another mate, only one, just you. Are you okay with that or do you want a relationship like your parents?"* I inquire.

"I don't want that, what would I do with another male?" I see her shoulders relax as she laughs at my wit. *"Truly I don't want to be like my parents, I want my own life, Draven. Their relationship is wonderful and I love my fathers'."* I see a timid smile grace her lips and it makes my heart jump. Tia blushes briefly then shyly looks down then back up to me. *"I don't know what to do with one male let alone many."* Tia trails off and I see her furrow her brows looking at me. She draws in a reassuring breath then smiles. *"You've said all I need to know, beloved. I will be cheering for you from the stands."* With a small nod and curtsey she turns back to the table where the family is.

I leave only once she is seated next to Ladon. I feel that she's at peace and calm at the moment, that in itself makes me happy.

SIX

LADON

Tournament day, hell yeah! Wow the last few days leading up to today have been insane. My sister and Draven are mates, I never saw that one coming. Up until they saw each other Tia was so laid back and now she's a nightmare with talons. Thankfully our Mom has her on a short leash for the matches that we have set up for today.

I make sure the thick black leather bracers on my forearms are tight and in the proper places. Gods know what we have in store for us today. I look over at Draven and he seems more focused than ever.

"Hey, you good?" I raise my brows looking at him, he's not acting like himself.

"Huh? Sorry, I didn't hear you. I was...distracted." Draven shrugs his shoulders like it was nothing. He still has that distant look in his eyes.

"I bet she's about five foot nine, has pale blonde hair and took down a Phoenix and a Dragon with permafrost. And also, she's my sister." I playfully punch Draven's shoulder. I look back up to the royal box waiting for both of our families to make their appearances.

Draven shakes his head looking at me then back up to the box. "Tia literally saved me from hell itself. She took out the psycho with barely any effort on her part, and she's my true mate to boot." Draven smirks then motions to the Royal box as everyone begins to take their place.

"She's so close, yet so far away." He lightly rubs my sister's scale as he watches for any sign of her presence. I've never seen him so taken by anyone in the time I've known him. It warms my heart knowing my sister will be well taken care of like she deserves.

Tia rushes to the edge of the box rail and looks down searching for us. Her face lights up the minute she see's where we are. The pale blue scarf around her neck blows gently in the breeze. Draven's scale is on full display with the dress she chose to wear for today. I can tell that mother helped Tia pick out the dress for tonight. It's an interesting nod to both her scale colors as well as Dravens. The gown is a bronze-gold in color with intricate silver-white details in the bodice. Tia looks more like the reigning Queen than the Princess that she is.

From here I can see the pale blue-white glow of her eyes as she focuses on us and then the arena around us. "She's proud of you, you know that? She never wears dresses that expose so much of her flesh," I say motioning to Tia. "She always wears high collars and covers as much of her skin as possible." I say enthusiastically

Draven is drawn to her like a moth to a flame. His eyes zone in on Tia then his scale. I see his skin ripple in an attempt to shift but he holds himself back. His Drake is definitely fighting him for dominance. I'll give it to him, he's got some serious self control. "Let's get this going before you combust, brother," I tell him, clapping him on the back.

ALMOST AS SOON AS Tia steps back Draven's mom comes forward and the crowd silences in moments. "Greetings Stormbringer Kingdom!" Queen Gisella announces.

"Thank you to those who have come far and wide to join us for this year's tournament. This is a joyous occasion not only to connect kingdoms far and wide but also to announce that my eldest son, Draven, has found his mate, Princess Tiamat Kraus." Gisella makes a sweeping motion towards Tia.

Hesitantly Tia steps forward at the mention of her name. "She is the heir to the Ice Dragon throne and only daughter born to Queen Aurora and King Consort Alaric Kraus." Gisella bows lightly to my parents and beams at Tia who's standing next to mother. Tia drops into a full curtsy after Gisella rises from her bow.

Slowly she moves to the edge of the booth and gently waves at all who is gathered. Tia's eyes lock on Draven and she removes her scarf, tossing it to him. Her hand raises and makes an arctic wind carry her token directly to him. Draven catches it in midair and holds it close to his heart enjoying my sister's scent, yuck.

"Now, to begin our first day, we are starting off with a labyrinth. Or maze if you will. This maze is no ordinary one. My mages have enchanted it in many ways to stop you from reaching your destination." She smirks before continuing. "You are not allowed to fully shift during this time. If you are caught you will be disqualified." She walks to the other side of the balcony.

"Day two consists of hand to hand combat with your weapon of choice, no magic is allowed to be used." Gisella's mood changes suddenly. "The final day is aerial combat, so you better bring your A game gentlemen!" She says staring down at Draven and I.

"We have healers on standby in the medical tent to provide aid to anyone in need. There are food and drink tents as well for your convenience for breakfast and lunch. Dinner will conclude our days in the hall."

"Let the tournament begin!" She says ending her speech.

DRAVEN HOLDS Tia's token in one hand and her braid in the other. "Brother would you help me place this properly? I'm not sure of your customs and don't want to insult Tia," He offers me my sister's long pale-blonde braid.

"Of course, it's my honor." I root through Draven's hair till I find the perfect spot for my sister's braid. I remove the waxed twine she used to tie one end of the braid and begin to weave Draven's hair in with hers. Once I am happy with what I've done I use the waxed twine to secure the braid in place with complicated knots. "All set brother." We fist bump and I back up smiling looking at how long my sister's braid is.

I see Draven weave Tia's token in his ponytail before making his man bun. Tia's braid sticks out like a pale blonde ribbon that's been twisted around the base of his man bun. I still don't quite grasp the concept but it suits him and his beard. The man is massive, well defined muscular physique and tattoos decorating his body. I'm not gay, but I can see why my sister finds him attractive, he's a good looking guy. Once Draven is settled, we head back to the tent and sort through our arsenal. We prepare by loading up with weapons for the labyrinth, who knows what we will find. Knowing the mages it won't be easy.

Heading out of the tent, Draven and I look at our competitors of all winged races and backgrounds. There are pure bloods, hybrids, dragon-kin as well as various other flight gifted species. This assortment of species ought to make things challenging.

Every competitor is lined up at the start of the Labyrinth and we wait for Queen Gisella to shoot off her lightning, signaling for us to begin. She rises from her seat and leans over the rail with her left hand raised. "Go!" she says as lightning erupts from her hand.

We take off without a second thought and head to the left moving over and around the obstacles. The mages really went all out, parts of the path moves while you're on it. We come to what looks like a huge divide, something doesn't feel right to me. "*It's an illusion. A leap of faith.*" I hear Tia's voice in my head and apparently so does Draven. He steps forward first and the illusion vanishes before our eyes.

I watch Draven raise his hand to touch Tia's scale as if to thank her before we move on. We dodge pit traps and vines that move of their own volition. The labyrinth is too tall to see over its walls, and the further we go the more the top closes over us. There goes our advantage of having Tia be our eyes. After breaking though the last vine trap we come to a Crone sitting on a stump waiting for whomever passes by. The path we are on seems to come to an abrupt end.

"Ma'am? Are you lost? Are you ok?" I ask her and take a knee before her. I was taught to respect and revere my elders, so I am doing that now.

"Such a sweet dragon you are. Don't you seek treasure young one?" It's now that she looks at me with milky-white unseeing eyes.

Okay, that's freaky. I school my features and draw in a deep breath. "My brother-in-arms and I seek passage further into the labyrinth. Do you have a test for us to pass to do so?" She's not sitting here for her health, there has to be a reason for why she's stationed here.

A smile plays upon her withered lips as she tilts her head to face my general direction. "Others saw me and turned around. Good to know that there may be some smart young men here after all. And a young lass from what I can smell." We watch her nostrils flair for a moment as she tries to identify our scents.

I look to Draven then back to the Crone. "It's the favor my sister gave to Draven that you scent ma'am, and perhaps the braid of her hair that's woven into his." Draven and I look at each other for a brief moment before looking back at the Crone.

The Crone starts to laugh. "Young love is so fleeting. Soon as a true mate is found that will be over in a flash." With a flourish of her hand a flame ignites then vanishes just as quickly to punctuate her point.

"I do have a riddle for you if you wish passage to the next inner circle. I do warn you. If you are wrong you will be sent to the beginning again." She says with a wicked grin, I'm slightly concerned by the way she's smiling.

Draven and I look at each other and then back to the Crone. "We accept the chance at the riddle ma'am," Draven says confidently.

"Hmm, two Dragon Princes are an interesting combination." The Crone states then adjusts how she's sitting. "In the harbor you see a boat full of people. It has not sunk, but when you look again, you don't see a single person on the boat. Why?" She finishes posing her question and then leans back, raising her glass and sips at her drink. She's giving off an aura of confidence, as if she believes we won't be able to solve the riddle.

I start to pace analyzing the Crone's riddle. "So there's a boat filled with people...," I trail off looking at Draven. He in turn draws stick figures on the boat so we have a visual.

We stare at the drawing. "It has not sunk, but you don't see a single person on the boat." Oddly enough Draven drew everyone paired up, I have a feeling he has Tia on the brain. "Draven you're a freaking genius! You drew the answer!" I slap him on the shoulder expressing my excitement.

Draven stares at his drawing puzzled then looks back up to me. "I did? What do you mean?" Draven raises a brow looking up at me after staring at his drawing again.

"Okay, okay...here look!" I point at the people. "Before Tia, when you would draw people on a boat they were all over the place. Now you have them paired up." Quickly I raise both of my brows up hoping he gets the hint.

Draven's eyes light up. "Is the answer that they are all mated pairs?" His hand rests on Tia's scale, as she unknowingly gave us the answer.

The Crone slowly stands and the illusion of being old fades away. Now she stands before us as a beautiful young elvish woman. "You're correct young Prince, you both may pass." She takes her slender hand and touches the wall behind her, the vines come alive and pull back. Beyond her seat is yet another part of the labyrinth for us to go through.

We push through the path as it somehow becomes narrower where we have to get in line and slide through the sharp leaves and vines. They are slicing through our arms like razor blades. Lucky for us we get out of the narrow spot and get to the wider opening in a few minutes. I use my frost flames to heal mine and Draven's wounds before we continue on.

WE DON'T SPEAK MUCH after that, but move forward finding a brick wall that resembles a puzzle. The pieces are all sorts of colors with white, blue, gold and bronze. What the fuck is this?

"I know what it is. We used to play a game when we were younger called madloone. We have to rearrange the pieces to make an image. Now, what that image is...is another story. Any ideas?" Draven asks me as he studies the blocks before us.

"The colors could possibly represent an image in our kingdoms? Kingdoms united?" I offer.

Draven looks contemplative as he considers my idea running his hand over his beard. "This might be a long shot but let's try it." He moves to shift the bricks and they move easily enough.

"What are you thinking it is?" I ask, watching him work.

"I think it's a dragon. You said kingdoms united and I'm thinking of the impending ceremony," Draven says.

"I can help guide you with the pieces. Move the bronze one down two spaces. Get the white one on the right, shift it up four spaces," I tell him.

We work in unison and accomplish our task creating a dragon out of the colored brick. As the last one slides into place our finish line is before us. Suddenly the line morphs before us into something indistinguishable—damn mages. I find myself staring at the shadows of two adults and two young children holding hands. What is this?

"Draven, what do you see?" I ask without looking at him. I'm mesmerized by what's before me.

"I see my future with Tia," he says in awe.

"Race you to the finish!" I yell at him and we both take off for the future we most desire.

As soon as we reach our images, they vanish into thin air. What is going on? What kind of mage trickery is this? There's nothing here, except...I smell a mage off to the side, blending in with the shrubbery.

"Do not be alarmed, Prince Ladon. You have completed your trial and are found worthy of a glimpse of your future as a small prize. It was not announced to be sure no one cheated. Take care." As soon as the mysterious Mage popped into my head, she left.

I shake my head as does Draven from what I see and then we both stare at each other bewildered. We clasp hands and hug as the crowd roars wildly. The labyrinth then disappears showing everyone who failed the task.

The two of us make a break from the madness erupting so we can get ready for the evening's festivities. The sunset is gorgeous and the secret prize has me excited for my future.

I MEET up with Draven in the hallway entrance to his family's wing. The man cleaned up nice for his mate wearing a dark blue button up, dark grey slacks and black dress shoes. Tia is going to go crazy because his long dark black wavy hair is down with her hair braided in still. The scarf she gave him is tucked into his shirt pocket with a small tail peaking out.

"Well...?" Draven asks with his arms wide. He's genuinely excited and concerned he doesn't look good enough for my sister.

"You don't look like an idiot," I say blandly.

"Thanks, *brother*. I feel the love," Draven says sarcastically.

"Anytime! Now let's go eat, I'm *famished*!"

I can smell beef Wellington and a spread of different smoked meats. I walk a little faster, as does Draven, we are always competing against each other. Once we enter the hall, Draven becomes mesmerized and stops in his tracks.

Shit.

SEVEN

TIAMAT

Even in my human form I have a delicate line of silver-iridescent scales that run from the nape of my neck to my tailbone. The line is approximately three to five armored scales wide following the length of my spinal column. The scales flare out at my shoulders and my hips in an intricate pattern. The blue dress I picked for today has the back wide open to my hips.

I decided to show off my anomaly tonight, grandfather says his grandma had the same scales. I've checked my twin numerous times over the years, not a single rogue scale. I feel like an oddity, but I love my scales and the unique look they give me.

After the boys had finished with the tournament I put my hair in a mermaid braid off to one side. I stand on the balcony with my hands on the rail looking out over Draven's family's Kingdom.

The expanse of land is green, with various colorful tropical flowers I've never seen before. Perhaps I'll ask my brother or my mate to take me for a walk. It's truly beautiful, but part of me misses the eternal winter of home.

I miss the pure white snow, it's cold embrace and the scent in the air just before a storm squall. My heart aches at the thought that I may never go home again. My mate may not survive the winters in Siberia. I must not think of just myself, this is a decision we will need to discuss together.

I can feel the boys approaching and sigh softly. My Dragoness is constantly at war with me lately. She's urging me to do things I've never thought of before now. On one hand, I don't wish to disappoint my parents and break protocol, on the other hand, I just want my mate. He's so close, yet far enough that when he walks away I feel a void.

Up till now, I never knew what I was missing until I finally looked into his emerald eyes and found forever. Growing up I was alone more often than not, now I have Draven for the most part.

I turn my head slowly to look over my shoulder, and see my brother and Draven standing there. "Congratulations gentlemen!" I turn slowly to face them and smile opening my arms wide briefly. "I'm so very proud of you both." I clasp my hands in front of me as I study them. My eyes shift for a moment then back to normal as I study my mate the best I can.

I notice that Draven has my braid in his hair. Tears well up in my eyes from the joy that I am feeling. I mouth *thank you* to Ladon knowing full well that he had to have helped Draven with it. My brother gave me a slight nod, then a wink.

I want to run to Draven and wrap my arms around his taunt waist. My eyes roam every inch of his masculine form. He looks like a dream made flesh. His suit is perfectly fitted like those lifetime movie princes wear. His shoulders are broad and thick, not hidden by his attire.

My eyes roam over the planes of his face, his rugged looks and well trimmed beard. I start to walk forward and stop abruptly, reminding myself of the proper order of things. I grit my teeth as a soft rumble from my Dragoness escapes my lips as I try to remain in control. It's now that I notice that Draven was studying me as much as I was him.

"I don't mean to stare but I can't help it. Your dress is bringing me to my knees before you but your eyes hold me captive. How did I ever get so lucky?" Draven says smiling broadly, almost proudly.

My face turns a deep crimson at his beautiful words. My heartbeat thrums in time with the pulse in Draven's neck and it takes everything in me to hold back from lunging forward. I study my mate more closely and flare my nostrils to attempt to catch my mates scent. My Dragoness is pleased by what little we can scent on the air, so she settles for now.

"I don't mean to break up the love fest but there is a delectable tray of meats making its rounds and I need to replenish, now," Ladon says, breaking our moment.

I roll my eyes at my brother, Gods he can be a real dick at times I swear. I steal a glance at Draven and move towards the table and pick a seat that has a chair on either side of me. Risky, yes...Gods be damned the next thirty-six hours is going to be hell on my poor nerves.

Draven seems to be rooted in place still staring at me. Do I have something on my face? I pull a small compact out of my hidden pocket in my dress and do a double check. My makeup is on point so I'm honestly not sure what's wrong with my mate. I'd ask him but I really don't want my overly perceptive brother to pick up on the fact I can hear Draven yet.

"Draven...are you hungry?" Ladon asks him as a double-sided question I'm sure.

"Excuse me?" Draven says. "I was lost in thought, you ass." Draven shakes his head slightly, trying to clear the fog.

Ladon hits him in the shoulder and we all take our seats waiting for the meat trays to come around. The wine is flowing and the feast is in full swing. I'm tempted to drink a little more than usual to calm me and my Drag-oness. If I do I might lose more than my inhibition tonight.

"You were wonderful out there today, you both were. There were so many who got taken by the vines and failed the tests." I giggle softly. "It was quite funny to watch and nerve-racking," I say digging into my plate of rare steak and potatoes.

"It was quite a task with the riddles and challenges. The oddest one was the end of the line. That gift was the best gift I've ever been given." Draven says with a hint of a smile.

"Pray, tell...what might that have been?" I ask curiously as I tilt my head to the side watching him closely.

"I was given a glimpse of my future. I saw you," he says leaning in towards me. My breath hitches in my chest at his words. I'm truly curious now.

RIGHT BEFORE WE get too close a brunette walks up and I feel myself go on the offensive to fight for what is mine. The scales on my spine and shoulders shift and stand on edge. My mouth opens on its own as my canines lengthen as I stare at the intruder.

"Hello, Draven." says the brunette in a sultry voice.

A low growl escapes my lips as a warning but this bitch doesn't seem to get the point. Slowly I stand up and move to the other side of the table to where the brunette is. Frost starts to coat everything I touch. Ladon is panicking but his voice sounds like it's underwater.

My mother stops Ladon with a single motion. I am of a singular focus, get the bitch away from my mate. My body feels like a live wire as the full extent of my power hums underneath my skin. Through our fragile bond I can feel Draven starting to get concerned and Ladon trying to soothe me. *Goddess be damned this bitch will not touch what's mine,* I growl in my mind.

"Hello!" I say in the most cheerful voice I can muster without being fake. I'm slowly moving closer to the bitch putting myself between her and Draven, in my head I hear my dragon's roar. *Torch her, turn her to ice. Kill the tramp.* My dragoness whispers in my head as my eyes remain locked with hers.

"Oh, hi, I'm actually here to see Draven. If you don't mind." She tries to push past me and I don't budge. I tilt my head left then right again assessing the possible threat in front of me.

I come to the conclusion that she is no threat, just some horny bitch looking to be with my mate. Over my dead body. "I do mind. I'm his *mate.*" I growl out the last part as I feel the frost creeping over my flesh. I quickly shift my arms to my armored gauntlets and click my talons together. She wants to play, I'll play...she touched what's mine once upon a time. In my mind she's dead, she just doesn't know it yet.

Just as I'm ready to strike I hear Draven call my name. "Tia! She's not worth it. Please, come sit with me, my love." I back away from the bitch just enough to get Draven in my line of sight. He has the chair next to him pulled out for me. I look between the female and my mate. The decision is easy, I go to Draven without a second thought.

But not without a final challenging growl and a small burst of frost in her direction. The female jumps back frightened, not expecting me to react the way I did.

My brother has the woman escorted from the room then puts my hand on Draven's arm. He gives Draven a terse nod and I feel the warmth of Draven's hand pressing against my bare lower back. I want to cry, I'm so happy.

I snuggle in closer, ecstatic that I've finally been granted contact with my mate. In the back of my mind I hear my Dragoness's crooning song. She sounds like a siren trying to lure a sailor to his death. I will have to be mindful more so now than ever. The mating ceremony isn't that far away now. To be honest, I can't wait.

EIGHT

DRAVEN

THAT WAS A CLOSE CALL WITH THE BRUNETTE. I don't even remember her name, only that she was a mistake. At least the girl had the decency to leave instead of staying long to be embarrassed further. I have to protect Tia and thanks to Ladon I'm able to provide her a small comfort.

My Dragon and I are more than happy to be this close to her even though it's not nearly close enough. I feel her relaxing as she shifts her gauntlets back and a smile with her blush being my reward. My hand rests on her lower spine and the scales there are cold to the touch, it's as if I have an ice cube in my palm.

We take our seats and I watch Tia fidgets restlessly with her hands. My touch has more of an effect on her than I realized. I lightly touch her bare arm and tilt my head offering for her to snuggle in closer if she so desires. Tia smiles and nods, hesitantly she leans against me. We are already pushing the limits as it is.

"Draven," my mother says, stealing my attention from my blonde beauty.

"Yes ma'am?" Slowly I raise my eyes to look at her.

"Preparations are almost complete for the ceremony." My mother states enthusiastically.

"Tia, are there any customs for your people I should be aware of? I'm curious to hear of your desires." My mother says smiling warmly at my mate.

"I would like to decorate a few items in frost, I'm sure mother will help you throughout the process," she says politely. "The only thing that matters to me, is Draven." Tia's eyes slowly drift from my mother back to me. The innocence that is my true mate is adorable with her pink cheeks and twinkling eyes. I swear I hung the moon for her and her for me.

Ladon rolls his eyes and starts eyeing up the females at the table. He then looks to his sister and smiles. "I'm sure you'll do fine. After all, remember who our great great grandmother is." He smiles and winks at her.

"Thanks, brother," Tia says before punching him playfully. Her eyes turn to my glass then back up to me. Slowly she extends her arm out and her index finger touches my glass. I watch a light sheen of frost coat it to chill the contents. Her eyes dart next to my mother's and she lays her palm flat on the table. A small steady stream of frost makes its way to mother's glass. Soon it too has been chilled. Tia carefully leans back against me again and beams up at me. She appears to be happy to do something so sweet and thoughtful.

Everyone at the table stares at the little trick she pulled. Mom is beaming at her and I'm tempted to place a kiss at her temple to say thank you but think better of it; my dragon is not happy. The other females on the other hand look a bit panicked.

"Thank you, daughter," mom says to her as if she were speaking to her own child.

My mother's acceptance makes Tia smile brightly from ear to ear making my flames roll over my skin and my scales become visible. Tia's eyes curiously watch my flames roll over my flesh. Quickly I extinguish them so as not to burn her accidentally. "Thank you, my love. That was incredibly sweet of you," I say holding myself back as much as I can.

"I'll do anything for you, betrothed," she tells me sweetly. "Are you okay?" She says, noticing my bronze scales. Tentatively she reaches out and runs her fingers over them.

"I am fine, only fighting temptation. I need to step out for a moment," I tell her as I struggle to remain composed in her presence.

She tilts her head to the side studying me for a moment. A sadness moves across her angelic features as she withdraws her hand. "As you wish betrothed, I'm truly sorry for causing any discomfort." Tia's eyes dart up to my mother then back to Ladon before she excuses herself from the table and walks swiftly back out to the balcony. I watch the area surrounding her coat quickly with ice. It seems her stress triggers a wintery reaction.

"I'm sorry brother," Ladon says softly as he motions to Tia. "Do you need me to go speak to her for you? I'm sure she just doesn't understand why you need to step away for a moment." Ladon looks down the table at the females then back again. "I'm sure the added stress isn't helping."

"No, it's okay, I can go to her. I needed to compose myself was all, nothing more." I say trying to get my lust and emotions under control. I excuse myself and find my way to my woman. I should be able to comfort her but as it stands, I will have to be careful. Watching my steps as I approach her, I draw a slow breath melting her ice.

"Tia...are you okay?," I ask timidly. If her Dragoness is in control I might get frosted.

"Did I do something wrong?" She asks with her head bowed and frost spreading across the rails.

"Baby, look at me. You didn't do *anything* wrong, do you hear me?" I ask, willing for her to turn around but she doesn't.

"My need for air was purely my fault because I was reacting to my primal desire for you. I'm at war with myself because my Dragon and I are one being." Sighing softly I lean my back against the rail.

"It's becoming increasingly difficult to not drop to my knees and worship you," I tell her, pouring my heart out, hoping she understands.

Tia furrows her brows looking quite puzzled. "Worship me?" She tilts her head several times. "I'm no Goddess that deserves to be worshipped." She sighs softly as she begins to pace.

I can feel the turmoil within her, she's in the same hell I am in. "Beloved? Do you know what it's like to not be allowed to touch anyone that's not family or one of my three guards?" She asks that question with tear-filled eyes. I shake my head no.

"Do you know what it's like to watch others give and receive affections freely? And not be allowed the same simple comfort?" Tia rushes towards me then stops within touching distance. She hesitantly starts to reach for me. Again I shake my head, my heart breaking for my innocent mate.

"Tiamat Andrea Kraus don't you even think about it!" Aurora bellows from across the room.

"*Enough!*" Tia roars back at her mother as she throws her arms out in front of her. Aurora is thrown back by the wave of frost that comes off of Tia. The look of shock on everyone's face is quite concerning.

"I've been good for so long, mother. I've done every single thing that you've asked of me." Tia shakes her head slowly. Time seems to be moving in slow motion as my mate begins to stalk her mother. The raw power radiating from Tia is intimidating, it feels as if she's projecting her Dragons immense presence in the room.

"Do you know what it's like to be attacked by all the dragons in the family? Just to give you time to sink your talons into my dragon-hide to put me into an ice sleep?" Tia's Dragoness is on the surface, I can see the scales ripple under her skin. Her hands shift to her gauntlets and she studies her talons. To think talons similar to hers being sunk into her flesh makes my stomach roll.

Tia stalks forward towards her mother. "Do you know what it's like seeing the pain in your twin's eyes?" Tia starts to gather frost in her hands. "Twenty years of heat cycles, twenty times I've been hunted and forced into hibernation. All because I matured ahead of schedule." She throws her hands up in mock surrender as she looms over her mother.

Aurora is crying softly having realized the pain she's going through. "I'm sorry Tia, forgive me."

Tia nods slowly then turns back to face me. Her hands shifting back to normal. "I want to know what a real hug is. I want to know what it's like to receive a kiss that's real." Tears slowly roll down her cheeks. "I will wait, but Goddess help the first person that gets in my way." She grits her teeth and bares her canines as she battles her Dragoness for control.

Tia's eyes are bathed in an ethereal glow as she approaches me. I open my arms wide just in case she is seeking the hug she so desperately desires. Her eyes move over my form and she sighs softly. Hesitantly she steps forward and into my embrace. Slowly I wrap my arms around her holding her flush to me. Resting my cheek upon the crown of her head my Dragon begins to rumble to her trying to comfort its mate.

Ladon the king of cock blocking gets in her line of sight. "Sissy, you need to eat." Tia blinks her eyes several times before breaking the hug. She looks between her brother and I, torn between duty and her mate. Softly she places a kiss on my chest over her scale before turning to walk away with her brother.

"Tiamat, wait." I say quickly.

She stops on a dime, turning to look at me with wide eyes. I close the distance between us and scoop her up in my arms and place a feather light kiss on her lips. Tia closes her eyes and leans into the pressure she's feeling from my lips. The amount of joy I'm feeling from her is immense. Slowly she opens her eyes and smiles at me. She pulls away reluctantly again. "Thank you my beloved, you have no idea how much this means to me."

"You're welcome, baby," I say, caressing her cheek. I'm happy to be able to give her at least a little comfort.

Sadly I watch her walk away as I stay outside. Once she's out of sight I jump from the balcony and shift. I need to cool off, I know the waters surrounding our kingdom will do just that.

NINE

TIAMAT

MY DREAMS LEAVE ME RESTLESS AND FILLED WITH sensations I don't understand. My heart races, and parts of me pulsed that have never done so before. I wake up close to midnight in a sheen of sweat. My body feels like Jell-O and I feel blissful. I wonder what could have caused that?

Hesitantly I reach up and touch Draven's scale and sigh. Whatever he did before bed got us both to relax. I'll have to ask him about it in the morning, and thank him profusely.

I can't go back to sleep right now, I feel the need to hunt for him again. I throw off my robe after I open my balcony doors. I run quickly and jump over the railing and shift as I fall. Normally I would roar as I take flight, but this is a secret mission.

This time I fly directly towards the ocean to hunt. I fly low over the waves covering miles of open water. A large fin breaks the surface of the water ahead of me. Perfect.

Immediately I dive and hunt the beast. The shark is used to being the predator not the prey. Tonight it shall be my singular focus, a gift to my beloved mate. Several attacks later I manage to sink my teeth into its thick leathery hide. It was no match for my Dragoness, then again anything less than a Tizheruk is a cake walk. I rip out its gills killing it almost instantly, quickly I sink my talons into its hide and start flying back to the castle. It's only a twelve-foot great white shark, but it's the thought that counts right?

It takes almost forty minutes before I make it back to the castle. Carefully I move the shark from my talons to my mouth and slide my present as quietly as possible onto Draven's balcony. A yawn escapes my maw and I decide to curl up in his courtyard and take a nap. To be perfectly honest, my dragoness barely fits out here, I move around knocking several shrubs out of my way before I curl up. I'll just close my eyes for a little bit, then I'll head back to my room before anyone notices.

Draven

THIS DREAM IS new to me, something has changed and I'm one hundred percent sure it's because I found Tia. The scenery is stunning with wintery weather, large moun-

tains and a miniature mansion. Outside of the home I see a rather large hill of snow and walk towards it wondering why it's out of place. I walk up to it slowly and warm it up to see what's underneath. It shakes and stretches snorting frost from its nose. A large yawn is released from its maw and I realize it's Tia.

"Well hello, my love," I say staring at her beautiful Dragoness. Her snow white and silver Dragoness is massive and heavily armored. If I remember correctly her twin isn't as armored as she is. My mate is literally a tank with razor sharp scales.

She looks more like a Silver Dragon than an Ice Dragon. Her horns on the top of her massive head almost spiral and are black on the tips. There's a frill that runs from the crown of her head to the tip of her tail. "I assume I've walked into your dream. I was thinking of you before I fell asleep." Tia shifts and I turn my back to ensure I don't sneak a peek although I'm dying to see her bare before me..

"Draven, beloved, it's a dream—I'm dressed," she says with a smile in her voice.

I turn around to see her in a stunning blue gown that barely hides anything from my curious eyes. I try desperately not to ogle her and keep my eyes trained on hers. I clear my throat to sneak a peek but stay inconspicuous.

"How did you find me here?" Tia says curiously as she slowly walks around her winter wonderland.

"I'm not sure to be honest. Like I said I was thinking of you earlier. Unconsciously I must have reached out to you in my dream and snuck into yours," I tell her with a smirk on my face. I know why I was thinking of her earlier... to release tension.

"I had an odd feeling earlier and I was at peace, far more relaxed than I have been in a long time," she says sheepishly.

"Oh? What did you do?" I ask her curiously.

"I, um...didn't do anything. It was more of what I felt," she tells me with red cheeks. So I nod for her to continue. "I felt a tightening in my lower abdomen and tingles down to my toes." Her hands trailed the length of her abdomen as she explained the feelings.

"My breath caught on a few occasions where it was almost hard to breath. I'm ashamed to admit but, I think I lost control of my lower extremities. I awoke to a puddle under my rear," she tells me as her whole neck turns red.

How can my mate be any more adorable? I knew she was sheltered and pure but...has she never attempted anything on her own? "Tia, baby, about what time was this?" I ask curiously.

"Around midnight or so, why?" She asks me with a tilt of her head. I know she is analyzing me.

"This might be hard to explain, and I'm quite shocked your mother never explained...," I trail off trying to explain the best I can without scaring her. I look her directly in the eyes continuing. "I was out of sorts earlier when I went on my flight due to how you affect me. I *didn't want to send your Dragoness over the edge by you scenting my shift in pheromones."*

"Why would you have done that?" She asks in a serious manner as if I meant to do it on purpose.

"I didn't want to do it but the things you do, the way you dress, your voice, your eyes...everything about you screams to me to mate with you, Tia." I state plainly trying not to confuse her further.

The ah-ha moment flashes across her face as she becomes shy and yet intrigued. I look down to my grey sweats and see how she is affecting me even now. Her sweet rain scent has been driving me mad since she left her territorial mark on Ladon to make sure the women kept their distance.

"How...does that work?" She asks me quietly, hesitantly pointing to my lower half with a wiggle of her finger.

"Well there...um...are a few ways. You felt the outcome earlier when I...attended to myself," I say bashfully. Damn it, this is harder than I thought.

"Can you explain? No one has told me anything, I have no idea what to expect. Please, Draven?" She all but begs me. I can tell she's nervous but curious in the same breath.

I take a deep breath and attempt to elaborate. "Well, females have reproductive organs internally as you know but men have them externally," I say looking down at the ridged outline of my cock. Carefully I use my hands to frame the outline of my member. "I was releasing my pent up energy by rubbing and stroking my cock," I say almost as if I'm a child with my hand stuck in a cookie jar, "I was thinking of you."

"You're going to have to be a little more descriptive, beloved, I don't know what a cock is besides a male chicken," she tells me in earnest.

"Well, you see," I start off, clearing my throat again, "a males extremity shape is that of a thick shaft with two ovaries underneath but we call them testes, or balls." I am trying not to laugh at this point because she is taking every word I say seriously. "At the top of the shaft is a mushroom shape where we can use the restroom from, or release...our semen," I manage to say finally. This is so embarrassing it's almost insane.

"So, you call your extremities your cock? Is a cock not a male chicken? You call your male parts a male chicken...why?" she asks in bewilderment. Tia furrows her brows looking at my crotch then back up at me. "Does it have feathers?"

I double over laughing as I sit in the snow, this is going to be a long night. "I am not precisely sure how it became that but there are various names for our parts. For instance there is; dick, one eyed monster, mushroom pole and many others that are vulgar." I can't believe she's made it this far and not seen a man naked. "No love, no feathers." I say attempting to be serious.

"So, let me get this straight...you stroked your mushroom pole and felt better after?" Tia tilts her head to the side, puzzled.

Suppressing another laugh I continue. "Well, yes. I had the urge to after seeing you at dinner, not to mention the way you smell. You are intoxicating and I will be happy to drown in your scent." I get a giggle out of that.

"To answer you better, what you felt earlier was me taking care of myself while thinking of you." I raise an eyebrow hopefully she understands. "The labored breathing, the electric tingles you felt, and the puddle you found under you...you were what I was doing for myself." This is probably the single most embarrassing moment in my life to date.

Tia looks a little mortified at that so I wait to see what other curious questions my true mate has. She opens her mouth and closes it a few times while pacing. I am quite lucky I have my internal heat source so I don't freeze out here.

"Draven...um, thank you, you know for the release feeling. It was euphoric to say the least." She flutters her hand in the air. "I didn't know what that was and now I do. What do you call it?" She asks now quite interested.

"It's called an orgasm, my love, and I am glad you enjoyed it," I say smiling.

"I want more knowledge, tell me more, please. How does our mating actually work?" she asks excitedly, still quite curious.

I snicker at that and decide I might as well tell her than it being a surprise on our mating night. "It might be uncomfortable at first."

"Why?" Her Dragoness is close to the surface again. Her eyes have shifted and swirl their liquid mercury.

"Because, my love, you are a virgin. You are pure beyond the word itself." I raise my brows trying to convey a relaxed manner. "I am going to be gentle with you until you are ready for everything else I have to offer you." I watch as her eyes shimmer into mercury and back again. Looks like I am making sense to one part of her at least.

"I will place the tip of my dick at your female entrance and move slowly upwards until your maidenhood breaks and allows me to move in and out of you with ease. I will worship your body so you do not focus on the sharpness but on the pleasure I will bring you." I say gently hoping that I don't frighten her.

I see her shifting her hips and her hands wringing together. I think I have caused enough pain for her tonight with all the teasing. The smell of rain is becoming over-powering, driving me mad. At this rate, I won't be sleeping tonight but we must rest for our big day tomorrow.

"We must rest, Tia. We can discuss more tomorrow, if you would like," I offer.

"I think I would like that," she replies with a little shyness.

"Go inside and get some rest, I will see your beautiful face in the morning." I blow a kiss in her direction and her face lights up. Completely worth it!

"Goodnight betrothed." She blows a kiss to me and I get a cold blast to my face then warmth as if she actually kissed me. This is pure torture.

"Goodnight." I say softly.

AFTER A LONG NIGHT of trying to reign myself in, I finally caved and wore myself out with back to back orgasms. I couldn't get the smell of her out of my nose. Now that I am awake I smell blood and a lot of it. I throw the rest of my covers off, and slip my pants on. I look through my opened balcony doors and see a great white shark dead with multiple puncture marks and its gills ripped out.

Next thing I know my bedroom door flies open and Ladon comes rushing in and pissed off with frost coating every step. "Well a fine good morning to you too, brother," I say confused.

"What the *fuck*, Draven. *Where is she?*" He yells at me, grabbing my shoulders holding back from possibly strangling me.

"What do you mean? Are you asking about Tia? What happened to her?" I ask, starting to panic.

"I can't find her and neither can anyone else!" Ladon says raising his voice and releasing me. "And what in the hell is that?" he asks, pointing to the great white shark.

"I think Tia left me a present again. I have to find her," I say, starting to panic.

"She was here...I smell her all over you! Don't lie to me!" Ladon practically roars. I know his anger is because he's worried about his sister.

"I wish she was here, but she's not!" I yell at him and take off towards the balcony ready to take flight to hunt down my mate when I see her Dragoness lying below. "*Ladon!*"

Ladon comes running and sees what I see. We both take deep breaths and, Ladon whistles to wake her and then launches himself off of the balcony down to Tia. I laugh at him, he's such a show-off.

"Draven, throw me your blanket please!" Ladon yells at me from below.

I jog around the gift Tia left for me and snag my throw off the floor and get back to the ledge and toss it down. Tia rustles finally to see Ladon next to her and she looks up to see me. I swear I see her giant maw smile. She stretches and takes a look behind her and quickly shifts allowing Ladon to wrap her up.

"Draven, when did you get a pond in your courtyard?" Ladon yells out.

"I di...I did it a little while back," I say. Tia looks red from here so I know she is embarrassed to all the skies above.

"Well, it's a nice addition. I'm going to get her back and ready for our day." Ladon says as he ushers his sister away.

I wave and let them go on their way. Let us hope he never finds out the truth.

Tiamat

OH MY GODS....I am so flipping embarrassed. I can't believe I fell asleep in Draven's yard and made a huge mess. Ladon thinks it's a new pond. I quit...I run my hands over my face trying to regain some semblance of calm. It's not working, I walk into my bathroom and turn the shower on and wait for it to heat up.

"Draven?" I reach out to him through the bond.

"Yes, my love?" Thankfully he answers swiftly.

"I'm so sorry...I'm so embarrassed. And of course, flipping Ladon had to find what I did, I just want to hide. How can I look at my brother again?" My anxiety is coming through loud and clear. I feel Draven lightly rubbing my scale to soothe me.

"Deep breath baby. He thinks it's a new pond, you're fine." Draven says gently.

"Are you sure, beloved? I can't believe what I did!" I practically shriek in his head.

"It's one hundred percent normal love, we all make moisture to different degrees when we have orgasms. Let's face it, your dragon is huge for a Dragoness. It was perfectly

proportional to her size." He tries to reassure me with facts.

"Ok beloved, if you say it's normal then I'm okay. Thank you for being there for me, Draven. I'll see you at break-fast." I say affectionately to him.

"See you soon baby." Draven replies.

I draw in a deep breath feeling a little better about this morning's debacle. I finally make it into the shower and enjoy the hot water. I ponder what dress to wear for today, but it really doesn't feel like a dress kind of day.

As soon as I get out of the shower I reach out to my mom through the bond. I hear her enter and leave my room quickly hoping she is dropping off something different for me to wear for today. Stepping out of the bathroom with my towel around my body, I walk out into my room.

There's flowers on the bed with a card, there's the faint scent of sandalwood so I know Draven sent them to me. I look over the white orchids mixed with black calla lilies. I smile and move the flowers and the vase to the table beside my bed. The card only has Draven's scent on it, I guess he rubbed it on his neck for me--awe.

Mom left me the black leather pants I requested as well as the bronze and gold bodice to go nicely with Draven's bronze scale. I pull my hair up into a high ponytail and give myself a once over. I paint my lips a deep crimson and only mascara on my long eyelashes. Then I spot the evil boots to go with the pants. Ugh, mom is trying to kill me, I hate shoes!

I carry the knee-high stiletto boots over to my bed and sit down looking at them. *Fucking shoes...*I say to myself. Sadly, the outfit wouldn't look right without the boots I don't think. I put on the tiny socks mom left with the boots and slid my feet into them.

Mom and I are almost exactly the same size everywhere, that is except in the breast department. I stand up with the boots on and take tentative steps with them adjusting to the five-inch heels.

Casually I swing past the mirror again to get a good look at myself. The bodice is barely containing my breasts. The heels combined with the leather pants make my ass look freaking awesome. Maybe, I'll start wearing heels more often.

I ponder the heels for a few more moments before returning to my dresser to grab the necklace that was once the Blood Queens. The blood ruby is absolutely beautiful and perfect in every way. I put the necklace on and grab the red silk shawl my mother left for me.

I exit my room and move silently through the halls trying not to draw attention to myself. Sadly a few of the male staff today seem to be quite clumsy dropping things all over the place. Maybe they're working too hard? I keep trying to adjust the ruby that keeps deciding to get lost in my cleavage. It seems every time I stop to dig it out something falls nearby. It's quite odd really. Maybe Draven would know why that's happening. I'll have to ask him when I see him.

I run into mom and dad on the way to breakfast and mom is ecstatic that I look so good in her clothing. Daddy dearest isn't thrilled at all and keeps suggesting that I put the shawl on sooner than later.

"Daddy?" I say and move to stand before Alaric. I look into my father's eyes and see unshed tears. "What's wrong Daddy, talk to me." I reach out and lightly touch my father's face.

Alaric leans forward and rests his forehead against mine and he sighs softly. "I'm so sorry for keeping you so isolated, baby girl. After everything your poor mother went though I was afraid of letting anything happen to you. Instead, what I did to you was far worse." Dad moves and kisses my forehead.

"Please forgive me Tia, I love you so much. Now my baby girl is going to be mated. I'm not ready for it." Daddy offers me the best smile he can while he attempts to get his emotions under control.

"Daddy, I love you so very much. I understand why you did what you did." I smile and kiss his cheek.

My eyes widen as the last of my father's words sink in and I panic a little. "Um, Daddy? Remember how you said you would answer any question of mine?"

My father smiles beaming with pride. "Of course my baby girl. What is that you wish to know?"

"So what happens after the mating ceremony? I mean I know Draven and I can finally touch more than a hug and a chaste kiss. But what else happens?" I smile looking forward to my father's wisdom.

Mom starts to cough, almost hacking up a lung. "Yes my love, what else happens?" mom says with a wicked smile. She leans in and kisses my father's now pale cheek then takes off running.

"*Aurora*! Don't you dare leave me!" Father starts bellowing as he runs down the hallway after my mother who just so happens to be laughing hysterically.

There you have it folks, my parents in all their glory. Mom told dad for years to let me out into the world but daddy said no... I can't help but laugh at the two of them. I continue on my path heading to the dining hall when I run into Queen Giselle. "Good morning your highness." I say as I curtsy.

"Tia you need not do that in private my dear." She smiles before hugging me and kissing my cheek.

"I'm so sorry there may be a challenge for your right to be Draven's mate, my husband didn't know you were enroute. I would never have allowed their invitation if I knew you were Draven's true mate." Gisella sniffles softly then blots away the rogue tears.

I return the Queen's affections and hold her hands. "It's truly fine. I will battle without issue. Besides," my eyes shift to that of my Dragoness. "They have no clue of my lineage, and it's about time they learn." I smile sweetly as I link arms with Gisella's.

"That's the fire this kingdom needs for their next Queen, not just some pretty face." Gisella says with a wicked gleam in her eyes.

"Father and mother both have been training me for battle for years. I will not be defeated." I say with utmost confidence.

Gisella nods slowly then motions to her private study. "Anything I need to know about the other contenders?" I tilt my head curiously.

"Well let's see, the three daughters from the clan Dimeter, are Green Dragons." Gisella shrugs her shoulders. "The daughter from the clan Wolferson, is a Black Dragon, she's almost four hundred years old and quite powerful." Gisella looks to me quite concerned.

"So, basically what you're saying is there's really only one contender." I shrug my shoulders. "I'll make sure to speak with my mother. After all she took down the Wyrm Black Dragon, Nexus." I watch Gisella's eyes widen.

"Yes, she would be the best teacher then, I suppose." She moves towards the door to exit. "Let's not keep the others waiting. After all, I cannot show favoritism daughter." Gisella winks at me then leaves swiftly. I wait several moments before heading down to join everyone.

DOWN IN THE DINING HALL, it is bustling with the competitors and visitors alike. I scan the area and make my way to where I see my family, Draven and his family. Gisella is in the corner speaking to the other contenders.

Draven drops his fork mid-bite and scrunches his nose a little like he's holding his breath. I know I don't smell bad, what gives? I walk towards them and I feel my chest jiggling and the ruby making its way down into my cleavage once again. I begin to fish it out and watch my betrothed eyeing my movements. His Adam's apple is clear to me as it bobs up and down slowly. I flash a smile and take my seat across the table from him.

"Good morning, betrothed. Did you sleep well last night?" I say, happy to see him.

"Indeed I did, and I woke up to a great treat this morning as well," Draven says as his dragon eyes make their appearance. What's got him on edge to have him shift like that?

"Excuse me, I think I'm full from my breakfast," he says and takes a napkin to wipe off his mouth and beard. He takes the napkin along with him at his side and I don't get why. Did he take food with him?

THEN IT HITS ME... I can smell sandalwood, the deep and rich scent taking over my senses as everything fades away and only Draven remains.

My Dragoness awakens and rumbles deeply in my chest. My senses are flooded with my mate's scent and I feel like I'm going to tear the world apart to get to him. Scales ripple up and down my arms, and I feel the bone plates in my face start to shift. My nostrils flare as my mouth pops open. I feel my canines descend and I'm practically panting. *Hunt him, catch him, make him ours...* My Dragoness purrs in my mind.

She spurns me into action, slowly I rise from my chair and start to stalk Draven. My Dragoness' eyes are focused only on him right now. I hear my family as if they are talking from under a pillow. My dragon's crooning song escapes my lips, seeing if she can appeal to her mate.

The next thing I know Ladon has his arms wrapped tightly around me and he's attempting to drop my temperature. I feel like my blood is on fire and now my brother is trying to stop me. I growl and snap at him, I don't want to hurt my brother but he's stopping me from what I desire most in the world. I know I can break free from Ladon, I know I can throw him...The mating ceremony is less than twenty four hours away, I can't take this anymore. Ladon is using his frost on me and I'm starting to get tired..*no*...I'm so close.

Draven is being held back from me by his father and it looks to be a struggle. I fight harder till my father lays his hands on me as well, assisting Ladon. I watch as Draven is dragged from the room by his father and at least three other men.

"Why...Ladon...I was so close...," I trail off as my eyes droop further and I am caught before I hit the ground.

TEN

DRAVEN

I can't help it, I have tried my best to avoid getting aroused when she is around but fuck me sideways that woman was on display today! The heels and the top... I have to stop thinking about her for a bit and kill something. I have to get her scent out of my nose too, nothing a little fire and smoke can't fix and maybe a few hand exercises.

"Draven, wait," Ladon says.

I spin around on my heals with my hard-on pointing straight at him.

"Whoa, put that thing away! You could hurt someone with that!" Ladon raises his hands as if to block my erection from his sight.

"I *can't*! You don't understand, Ladon. Not yet at least." I say rubbing the side of my shaved head. "I don't say that to be mean, I don't know that I can wait another night.

I'm dying over here and I know she is too." I shake my head trying to clear it.

"I saw her trying to get to me as hard as I was trying to get to her! We're going to go crazy. We have to stay away from each other until the ceremony." I say desperately, my voice tinged with the remorse I feel knowing it's what's best.

"I understand, that's why I was heading your way. I think it will be best to keep you two apart until tomorrow." Ladon sighs, looking sad. "Tia will be asleep up to six hours and she will be fine. She is not happy with me right now, but she will be okay." Ladon moves around uncomfortably "I know she will want to see the competition. Now will you *please* handle that monstrous thing!" he says exasperated motioning at my groin.

I move quickly to my room, sealing the door behind me to avoid my scent leaking into the castle. I don't want to cause any more discomfort and I hope that this will relax her as well as me because I am wound up so tight, I might combust soon.

I strip down and get to business thinking of her long pale blonde hair spread across my bed. Her ample breasts moving ever so slightly as my mouth descends on her body. I want to lick and taste every piece of her. *Shit*, that was a fast release.

I MAKE my way down to the grounds and get ready for the tournament. Ladon comes popping out from around a corner and almost gets a face full of fire. "What the fuck man! You know I'm on edge!" I yell as I try to settle my rapidly beating heart.

Ladon rolls his eyes then looks around all shifty. "You need to see this...here put my hoodie on to help cover your scent."

I stare at the offered sweatshirt and slip it on. Then proceed to follow him back into the castle and through the halls to his parent's room. I give him my best what the fuck face I can and he fucking shooshes me. We walk out onto the balcony and now clearly I hear the clashes of swords.

Ladon motions to the one huge cedar shrub he placed in the corner and the chair near it. I take my seat and look in the yard. Tia is sparring with her father full force and neither shows any signs of holding back. This is probably one of the coolest things I've gotten to witness.

Alaric is rumored to be one of the dragon's greatest swordsmen and my mate is driving him back. I'm so very proud of Tia watching her force her father to go on the defensive. Out the corner of my eye, I spot Aurora leaning on the rail watching her daughter fight.

"You know you have your talons full with that one right?" Aurora says then smirks. "I almost feel bad for you. Then again Austin told us how much of a handful you are as well." Aurora moves closer to my hiding place.

"She's incredible," I whisper hoping the sound of the swords clashing conceals my voice. I can't take my eyes off my mate for more than a few seconds.

"That she is." Aurora takes her cup of coffee and sips from it. "It hasn't been easy for her, she matured so young." Aurora sighs. "I suspect it was about the time you did. There's what, three years difference between the two of you? That would make you about twenty eight-ish?" Aurora raises a brow looking at me.

"Yes, your majesty, I'm twenty-eight, I'll be twenty-nine in a couple of months," I whisper my answer.

"Talons and gauntlets, ice weapons allowed!" Aurora suddenly bellows, my eyes widen in shock as I watch the swords get thrown to the side.

Tia and Alaric go to their respective sides having heavy leather armor being applied to their chests and necks. What the fuck am I about to witness? Aurora is relaxed while Ladon is chilling out looking bored. I guess this is the status quo for their family. Ladon moves closer to me and smirks. "Don't stress, Tia hasn't lost against father in almost five years. This is more for a distraction for her than anything else," Ladon says softly.

"She could have ripped free from me last night easily, but she chose not to. Mostly because she feels guilty for hurting me every time we have to put her under." Ladon schools his features quickly.

"I feel guilty for having to attack her and help mother get a shot at her." He looks down briefly then back up to me.

"If I would have known sooner that she was yours, I would have brought her to you," Ladon says, sounding remorseful.

I lay a hand on his shoulder to show him comfort. I know he would have, he doesn't need to explain. I return my gaze to my mate fighting her father. Tia's gauntlets look more aggressive than Alaric's, and her talons are longer.

"Is he going to be ok against her?" I ask.

Ladon smirks then motions to his mom. "Worst case scenario, mom jumps in and ends it, or battles Tia herself." Aurora winks at me as I peer at her over Ladon's shoulder. Ladon whispers. "Tia can defeat mom, it's not common knowledge so shh.." My eyes widen at the news, Aurora is known to be a phenom in battle. To know my lithe mate can defeat her mother just rocked my world.

The surrounding temperature starts to drop quickly and I look back at the battle below. They are hurling volleys of their ice weapon at each other like kids would snowballs. I think I've landed in an alternate universe. Alaric suddenly shifts to his dragon and stares down at Tia. I get ready to launch myself between them when I feel a cold hand land on my shoulder.

"Watch." Is all Aurora says to me and motions back to my mate.

I hear Alaric's ignitor click and a steady stream of fire rains down on Tia. My heart just about stops. I feel her through the bond, and she's fine. It's now that I notice my father and mother off to the side watching. Alaric's flames stop and Tia is standing there covered in her dragon's scales. I can only see her backside from this angle but what I can see is stunning.

My mother is standing there with a robe in one hand and a ball of her lightning in the other. Tia gives her a nod, and promptly she's hit with my mother's lightning and fire. I don't feel any pain, nothing. Aurora leaps over the balcony and helps Tia slip her robe on then leads her back inside.

My stunning mate is *fucking immune* to a storm attack, thank the Goddess above! I feel a tug on my sleeve and I look at Ladon. "Time to go, Mom wanted you to see that even though Tia isn't worldly, she can handle herself in any situation."

WE GO BACK to our rooms and I find my father standing on my balcony with his back to me. I wonder what's going on with him, I'm getting a vibe off him that tells me this won't be a pleasant chat.

"Hello, son," Father says to me as he turns around.

"Hello, father. What brings you by?" I say curiously.

"I want to talk to you about Tiamat," he says rubbing his head awkwardly.

"Please tell me this is not the swords and sheaths conversation," I say with a groan. "You do know I am twenty-eight, right?"

"I know that son, but Tiamat is different. Alaric kept her under literal lock and key to protect her. I know you saw her fight earlier, and she is a formidable opponent. Your mother would have to use mages to siphon her powers to possibly win the fight and that's playing dirty," he says flustered.

"I know and she is everything and so much more than I could have ever imagined," I say passionately.

"I understand and I feel the same way about your mother. I want to warn you though...she might tear you up--literally." Father says concerned.

"Dad, really...I know. It's not as if I haven't done it before," I say before biting my tongue.

"Yeah, that's what I am worried about. You better not let it slip that you've taken another's purity. Tiamat will hunt that poor girl and annihilate her. She already killed Raven and Janel, their parents understand, but are heartbroken." Father says raising both eyebrows high trying to get his point across.

"I won't say a thing. Will you pass on my apologies to their parents?" I slightly bow my head out of respect for the dead. "I will keep my thoughts to myself about her personality change. You and I both know my life would have been hell had I been paired with her," I say with a hard exhale.

"Yes, son. Now, go kick some fucking ass in that tournament and show your mate how strong you are!" My father says as he claps my shoulder and makes his exit.

I shut my door behind him and make my preparations for the tournament.

LADON and I armor up and get down to business. Metal against metal and without magic, I miss these fights, especially with the fae and the ogre's--it gets my blood boiling. My draconic side wants to go tear into another apex predator and gift it to my woman as she did for me. After the tournament that is what I will do, but I will find her something delectable to appease her Dragoness. Actually, I think I'll do it for our honeymoon.

"Are you ready to do this, brother?" Ladon asks as he motions towards the arena.

"Yeah, I'm more than ready," I tell him with a wink and slash my long sword at him.

Ladon jumps back and hits me in the shin with ice, the jerk. We laugh as I melt it and head out to the grounds. The arena is roaring with people from everywhere around the supernatural community. I see Tia in the stands with her hair braided in a crown around her head and a stunning black lace v-neck with leather pants. She looks lethal and ethereal as she waves to me in true princess style.

I raise my sword to her and the crowd roars even louder. My mother stands, waiting a minute for the crowd to settle then motions to her mage to magnify her voice.

"Good day everyone and thank you for joining us! We expect to see everyone in the tournament put up a good fight not only for themselves but for our spectators!" Mom says excitedly.

"As a reminder, no magic, and only partial shifting is allowed during this time. This is *not* a fight to the death... the goal is to showcase your abilities. With that said, let the combat trials *begin*!" With a flick of her wrist lightning bursts in the sky and we begin fighting our paired up opponents.

We pair off to our first round opponents and lucky for me I am up against one of our guards, Zaylen. I know his moves inside and out, this will be easy. We dance around with our swords clashing and driving him back to a defensive stance. Driving onward I slice toward his chest but miss as he rolls away.

I move quickly to kick him in the face to knock him out but he jumps up faster than I realized and takes a swing at my torso. I jump back in order to avoid his sword and take a direct hit. I slash out at him to drive him back once again, as our swords clash together I swing his arm out to the right disarming him and pointing my sword at his throat. He nods to me slightly signaling his defeat.

I hear the crowd erupt at my victory and I search the stands to find Tia clapping along with my parents and hers. I move on to another area to find Ladon in a hand to hand combat. Ladon has his arms positioned like a well trained boxer as he bob's and weaves to avoid his opponent. He ducks down and in a flash, he jabs upwards with his right hand into his opponent's gut. Then with his left, he hits the guy across the face knocking him out. I clap slowly and wait for him to come over so we can recover in our tent together before the next round.

"You did well, brother. That was a pretty swift jab to his head. I'm sure he will be feeling that," I tell him chuckling.

"You bet he'll feel that. I also heard you won yours, as to be expected. I am shocked I heard the roar of the crowd over all of the fights that are taking place around us," he says.

"They did go a bit nuts, didn't they? Usually it has a more profound effect on me but the only one who has that effect is Tia." I look back up to the royal box where Tia is.

"All right you lovesick fool, focus on the battles. You can focus on her tomorrow," Ladon says messing with me.

We get back to our tent and prepare for the next round of fights. I pull out my favorite pair of hunting swords. They are forged from seven hundred folded damascus and sharpened to a razors edge. The hilt is made of basilisk tooth and gold inlay. I test the weight of my swords and twirl them several times before slashing at the air with them.

"Draven, are you sure you want to pull those out now?

You are deadly with those and your mother did say that this is not a fight to the death," Ladon tells me as he walks by to pick out new weapons.

"I want to make sure that I show off my best assets," I say with a grin.

Ladon only rolls his eyes at me then picks up his weapon of choice—a spear. I raise my eyebrows in question but he only shrugs his shoulders while playing with his new toy. We make it back out to the grounds for the second round. Our eyes move over the brackets to see who has made it to the finals along with us.

The field has narrowed by half at this point. Some of the battles we were hoping for just aren't going to happen this year. The board shows that my next opponent will be Orxan. His background proves worthy of our fight due to him being a phoenix and private guard for the wealthy.

"I got some scrub from another kingdom," Ladon tells me.

I chuckle as we head to our places. This ought to be interesting—and it was. I've made it through my battles to the finale. Ladon just lost to this massive black dragon that goes by Jurgen. The man is immune to ice and pulled a stunt on him to win.

"You think he's cheating too, don't you?" Ladon asks me.

"Yeah I think but I'm not picking up on anything magical. I'll have to investigate when we are on the field," I say. Ladon clasps me on the back wishing me luck as I enter the arena.

Tia makes her presence known as a chill crosses my cheek. I shift my arm letting fire pour out into the sky creating a bouquet of roses.

The deafening roar of the crowd comes to silence as Jurgen makes his entrance. His human shape is that of a powerlifter but his head looks to be deformed or mutilated with odd features. We meet in the middle, touch swords and begin our battle. My hunting sword's clash with his as we exert our full strength at one another. Our feet dig into the ground, unwilling to budge.

My left knee comes up to nail him in the ribs and I hear a satisfying crunch of bone. It may not be a deathmatch but I can have fun inflicting some pain. Jurgen takes a few steps back with hatred in his eyes as he rushes me, catching me off guard.

I hit the ground hard realizing his fist didn't hit my chest, the hilt of my sword did along with my blade embedded in his shoulder. I roll him off of me waiting for him to surrender to me. I slightly turn my back to him to look at Tia when I feel the sensation of a sharp blade tearing into me. The bastard shoved it from the back of my knee up through the top of my thigh. I swiftly turn around and kick him in the face rendering him unconscious.

Everyone in the stands goes insane with cheering but I feel like I'm losing consciousness. Voices are becoming muffled and I can't see anything clearly. I feel my body drop to the ground and the blade twist into me. I feel Tia in the back of my mind screaming before I lose consciousness.

Tia

THERE'S those scenes in a horror movie that time slows and you see every intricate detail. I watch the blade pierce Draven's skin and instantly I start feeling the strength drain from him. Whatever that blade is coated with, is killing him.

"Mom, Draven's dying...forgive me." I leap out of the box falling fast towards the ground. I put my hands out in front of me and create a large snow mound to cushion my fall.

"Ladon! Get the blade out! *Hurry!*" I watch my twin leap into action as I sprint towards them. I skid to a halt a mere feet away from Draven, his skin is ashen and he seems to be losing the battle against whatever that blade was coated with. I can heal him, I know I can.

Queen Gisella and her mage arrive on the scene and identifies the toxin on the blade, I was right it's what's killing him. "Can you conjure a blanket that would be immune to my frost flames. I'm going to heal my mate." The Queens mage concentrates and creates the requested blanket for me.

"Ladon, wrap Draven up tightly in the blanket leaving only his leg exposed. When I shift, lay him in my taloned hand." It makes my chest hurt to have to move away from Draven but I must do this. I shift to my Dragoness quickly and lay my thick tail over the male that hurt my mate. I'll deal with him later.

I lower my head and whine at my brother as I lay down offering my taloned hand for him to lay Draven in. My mate doesn't have long, I feel him slipping minute by minute. I throw my head back and roar before I lower my head to gently blow my frost flames on Draven's leg. I am focusing all of my love and power into my bright blue flames. I don't hear anyone anymore, I just hear Draven's heartbeat. It's slowly becoming stronger the longer I breathe the flames upon him. I watch his skin start to regain color and his breathing starts to even out.

I hear a deep growl type groan come from Draven and my heart stops. He's not only the most beautiful male I've laid eyes on but the voice does things to my insides.

"My love...," Draven whispers weakly.

I whimper because I want so badly to nuzzle him. I lower my muzzle to him and gently press it to his body drawing his scent into my nostrils. Under my tail the male that hurt my mate is starting to move. I pick my head up to look back at him briefly, turning back I look at Draven.

"End him," Draven tells me.

Queen Gisella nods in agreement with her son. That's all the permission I need as I lay him down and have his mother and father tend to him. I stand up to my full height and stretch my Dragoness out.

Carefully I place myself between my mate and the asshole that tried killing him. I lower my massive head and growl at the male as he rolls to his feet. I don't think he was expecting to see a massive hybrid like me. The body of a Silver Ice Dragon with some features of a Wolf. I blow some permafrost on the ground in front of him as a warning shot. Snarling I bare my teeth at him allowing a deep menacing growl to escape my maw. My twin tells me that they are clear and in the tunnels far enough away.

I roar at the man sending him flying backward, just before impact he finally shifts. Oh my day just keeps getting better and better. His Black Dragon is barely half my size, the whelp doesn't know who he's fucking with.

I hear his ignitor click and before he can fire I blow a blast of permafrost at his throat. It freezes his flesh solid, no matter how hard he tries he can't release his acid breath. The bastard charges me and bites into my armored hide getting mostly a mouthful of fur.

My guard, Marco, taught me how to go head to head against a Black Dragon. One of the best lessons was that their scales are not as tough as mine. I rear up and sink my talons deeply into his flesh, I manage to sever a wing from his back and open his side up. His blood pours out all over the arena floor, but that hasn't stopped him from trying to attack me. I back up and launch back at him again going after his other wing. I manage instead to get my maw around the back of his neck just at the base of his skull.

Quickly I start thrashing my head back and forth feeling the muscles and tendons ripping as my taloned hands keep pushing his body down. Several thrashes later I rip his head free of his neck. Blood sprays wildly from the exposed arteries in his thrashing wound. His body begins to make spastic movements coating the arena in his blood.

My once pure silver-white scales and fur is painted vermillion. I open my mouth one last time to pick up his head. Carefully I carry it over to the tunnel that holds my mate and I lay it down before him and our families. I scoot back slightly and lay down resting my massive head on my taloned hands waiting.

Queen Gisella looks pleased as does Austin. Draven is beaming at me though he is still weak. Pride doesn't begin to explain what I am feeling along with relief.

"I'm quite disappointed to announce that after your show of force the other suitors left quickly." Gisella smiles at me then motions to her mage.

"Tia, if you will allow me...may I take your sense of smell as a reward for the night? I will take Draven's as well. I want you two to be able to court tonight and enjoy your time together without any complications," she offers. "I will give it back right before the ceremony."

I tell my brother through our bond that I am happy to do so and he tells her for me. I watch her motion to her mage. His eyes glow eerily white as he approaches my maw. The next thing I know, I can't smell anything at all-- what a strange sensation.

"Thank you, mom," Draven says as he stands up with his father's assistance.

"One more thing Tia, as a wedding gift may I connect your clothing to your shift?" Gisella says to me smiling, she is absolutely beaming with pride.

I blink my eyes in astonishment then nod my head in agreement. I watch her closely as I feel a tingle wash over my body making me shiver. I see her smile grow and my tingles stop. I hope this works or everyone will be getting a show they won't forget. I look from Gisella to her mage and he gives me the thumbs up.

I RISE UP and walk away from everyone just in case this doesn't work. I turn my back to our family and close my eyes concentrating on shifting back. Unfortunately for me, my shift has always been slow. I focus and draw it out even longer than usual being mindful of if there is or is not any clothing.

Several minutes pass and I finally open my eyes, apparently Queen Gisella favors me in gowns. It's a beautiful blood-red gown that's floor length and flares at my hips. My ample breasts are well contained and are modestly covered. I turn slowly and begin to walk back to the group. I drop into a gentle curtsy and smile. "Thank you for this thoughtful gift Mom. I greatly appreciate it." I run my hands over my gown then look to Draven to see if he approves. His broad smile tells me it's an instant hit.

I know my mate is weakened from the poison so I offer him my hand. Draven smiles and limps over to me and takes my hand gently. My eyes drift to both sets of parents. None dare to say anything to me right now. I just took out a Black Dragon on my own and avenged my wounded mate. My mother has tears in her eyes and she keeps saying "My baby did that!" as she points to the males head on the arena floor.

This death doesn't phase me like the first two did. It kind of concerns me that it's not bothering me. Draven and I walk hand in hand down the hallway and back into the main part of the castle. Ladon is at my side and is waiting to escort me back to my room.

"Before I go, my love...," Draven says in a deep voice. "Will you allow me to kiss you?"

My heart pitter-patters rapidly, I love that he asked permission. I nod shyly and watch him approach. His hands glide up my arms and then one moves to cup the back of my neck. His fingertip plays with the scales at the edge of my hairline. We inch closer together closing the distance between us.

The gentleness that touches my lips along with the heat causes scales to ripple along my cheeks. I feel a slight shift in the bone plates in my face as I reign my Dragoness in.

Draven's lips are softer than I had expected. I always imagined a man's lips to be as hard and unyielding as his muscles. Pleasantly I'm surprised. The bone plates in my face keep trying to shift and realign.

Curiously I raise my hands to caress Draven's beard and cheeks. I'm shocked to discover that his facial plates are also trying to shift and realign like mine are. Reluctantly I break the connection as I start to feel the tingle in my nether regions. I blush and look down and away. "I went too far. Forgive me?"

"There is nothing to forgive, my love," Draven says breathlessly. "I cannot wait to make you mine." The growl that escapes him makes me shiver, I want that so badly.

"We need to get going or I'll break every rule in our kingdom." He says desperately, I know he's as on edge as I am.

I giggle at his inflection and nod. Both of us go our separate ways and get ready for the feast tonight. I stay for a moment and watch him walk away admiring his physique. Draven must feel my eyes on him as he looks over his shoulder and winks at me. My cheeks turn crimson as I tuck my head slightly.

I take off to my room and brush my teeth, after all my last meal was grimy. Admiring my outfit I chose to keep it on and only fix my hair, nothing more.

I hear a knock and Ladon enters my room. "Wow, sissy, I think you need to spray some perfume first," he tells me, pinching his nose.

I look at him like he's an idiot then smell my underarms but nothing, only my scent of rain. I don't even smell Ladon. "What is wrong with the way I smell?" I ask in irritation.

"You smell...*potent*," he retorts.

"I can't smell a damn thing you ass! Stall for me I'll go shower and hopefully that helps." just for good measure I hit Ladon with a blast of ice, bloody hell I forgot that Gisella took my sense of smell.

I'm wound up tighter than a top. I swear to the Gods that if this night doesn't pass quickly I may just raze this kingdom to the ground if they keep us separated much longer. I think I spent the better half of thirty minutes scrubbing myself from nose to toes if this doesn't help, I don't know what else to do.

I walk from my bathroom to my wardrobe in my fluffy robe and search for an outfit for tonight. There's usually dancing at the feasts so I search for a dress that will cover enough skin that if Draven asks me to dance I can. I found the one my grandfather's mate Helle had made special for me.

The gown is covered in iridescent sequins that are similar in color to my scales. I slip it on and fasten the collar around my neck. This particular dress has a full back, as well as most of my chest, is contained. There's a small cut out section above my cleavage that allows Draven's scale to be seen. After digging through my bags I find my mythril tiara that Oberon made for me himself. The tiara

itself appears to be made in the form of delicate
snowflakes. Within the snowflakes, diamonds and other
precious jewels. I had allowed my hair to air dry and curl
naturally.

Carefully I sit the tiara upon my head then look at myself
in the mirror. I reach out through the bond to Ladon and
request for him to escort me to the feast. With the possi-
bility of dignitaries and allies to Austin's and Gisella's
Kingdom possibly being here it isn't proper for a
betrothed female to be unescorted. It's about time the
Stormbringer Kingdom gets properly introduced to the
Winter Princess.

Several moments later a knock sounds at my door and
Ladon enters wearing his pale grey suit with an iridescent
handkerchief in his pocket, my brother knows me too
well. After the show I put on in the arena I didn't want
anyone to forget who I am and what I can do. I place my
hand on my brother's forearm and allow him to escort me
to the feast.

ELEVEN

DRAVEN

My nerves are getting me hyped up as I shower roughly. I'm anxious to get back to Tia so I can hold her hand again. For being so innocent she sure can illicit a reaction from me like no one ever has. Lucky for me though mom took our sense of smell so she can't pick up on me. I finish up, wrap a towel around my waist, and pick out a nice pair of black slacks with a silver dress shirt.

I heat up my head and watch my hair dry along with my beard. I spruce up and put a few products in to tame the wave I got from my mother's side. I splash some cologne on, toss my dress shoes on and make my way downstairs, eager to see my mate.

Jogging my way down and into the dining hall I search for her but I don't see her just yet. Good, I want to give her a surprise. I head straight back to the kitchens greeting everyone I see. I find a large block of ice and take it to our table, placing it in the center of the table in front of me. I use the fire from my pointer finger with laser precision and cut out a massive bouquet of roses for Tia. I finish in time to see her and Ladon enter the room. I look at her, then to my masterpiece grinning. I hold my hand out for Tia to take and have a seat as Ladon sits next to Tia's other side.

"Draven, it's beautiful! Thank you!" Tia says bashfully as she touches the sculpture.

I feel her in my chest and touch her scale applying a little pressure to it watching her blush. I take my seat next to her holding my hand out again, palm up so she can rest her hand in mine. The slight pressure of her hand is enough to make me take in a sharp breath.

"I know they aren't real flowers so I was hoping you would like them." I say hopefully.

"I love them. Were you making these?" she asks in wonder. Nodding my head I answer her question. Her face changes to one of happiness to concern. "Are you healing well? I lost it when I felt you get injured and fading. It tore me apart." Her eyes shift to her dragon's and I feel the rage bubble to the surface. Tiny silver scales surface on her eyelids and around her eyes as she watches me intently.

"I know you did, I felt your panic and I am truly sorry for that." I look down briefly then back up at her." It's been a very long time since anyone has gotten the upper hand on me like that." I drop my head for a moment, before looking up to her again. "I'm glad you are okay too. Even though you are as powerful as you are, I was worried sick," I tell her, rubbing her hand with my thumb.

"When it comes to protecting you, I'm not afraid of anyone or anything, beloved," Tia tells me as she squeezes my hand tightly. I can almost swear I can feel her power buzzing just under the surface of her skin.

"And I you." I say with conviction.

"Can you two stop being all lovey for a few minutes? I would like to be able to eat my dinner," Ladon pipes in reaching for his mug of beer.

Tia has a little twinkle in her eye and freezes Ladon's drink solid. He gets hit in the mouth with a block of ice. We both erupt in laughter and I toss a flame into his cup as he puts it back on the table keeping his beer chilled but thawed out.

"Very funny you two, maybe this relationship isn't what we need for the kingdom's after all," Ladon says as he rolls his eyes, jokingly.

"Soon enough dear brother, you will have your own mate creating your own fun at us," Tia says sweetly.

We enjoy each other's company and our parents for the duration of our dinner. Pit fire pork is served with a multitude of other roasted dishes. My favorite is the roasted spaghetti squash with the green beans and bacon. I wonder what Tia's favorite is.

"Tia, my love, what is your favorite dish tonight and of all time?" I inquire.

"I love all sorts of meat, rare or raw meat that is," she replies.

"Well, that is to be expected. I assure you I won't cook your meals with my fire...unless you ask nicely," I tease. "I particularly like my deserts heated."

"*Draven*! Really, man, I do not need to be hearing this. I'll be stepping out for a moment. mother and father can watch over you for a moment," he announces and takes his leave from the table.

"I think he is jealous and grossed out," I tell Tia.

"I do worry about him though. Hopefully he finds his mate, like I have found you." Tia lightly touches my shoulder with her free hand. "We also have a lot to be thankful for with Ladon. Had it not been for him, we might never have found each other," she says with a small tilt of her head.

"Ladon has always been a brother to me ever since we were kids and that won't change now. He will stand with us as my best man at our ceremony," I say. "Who will be standing with you tomorrow, my love?"

Tia sits there pondering the question, she starts to get antsy in her seat. She looks anxiously at her mother and I can feel the tension and sadness rolling off of her.

"Tia baby, what's wrong? Tell me so I can fix it," I implore her, holding her hand tightly.

I hear someone get hit and I look up to see that Aurora had hit Alaric's bicep. "This is your fault." Aurora whisper yells at Alaric.

"Momma no, please." Tia sniffles and draws in a deep breath before turning to face me. She straightens her back and sits up straight.

"I have no one." She looks back up to her parents and then back to me.

"Myself and my sister Kirra were kept separate from most of the world. We are the last females born of both families with the right to title." She smiles looking down at her double crescent moon birthmark.

"Ladon has been everything to me all my life, I'm glad that he is your best friend. At least I will never lose him." Tia raises her free hand and taps a finger to her chin thoughtfully. "As for tomorrow, I think I will call for my sister Odette to stand with me." She forces a smile as I watch her eyes take on an ethereal glow.

Slowly Tia stands and walks over to Aurora. "Momma, I need a boost," Tia says as she offers her hands to her mother. Aurora takes hold of them and both of their eyes glow white. A slow smile spreads over Tia's lips and I can feel her joy.

"Edgar is bringing her posthaste, they should be here late tonight." Tia kisses her mother's temple before returning to sit with me.

"She can sleep with me tonight Momma, I do so miss our sleepovers." Tia smiles up at her mother then looks back at me.

"My sister Odette is a Great Bear like Papa Dimitri," she smiles broadly, "or as I like to call him, Papa Bear." Tia giggles like a little girl as Aurora shakes her head at her.

"You do realize you got all the other daughters calling him that and they all get away with murder now as well," Aurora says smiling affectionately at Tia.

Tia giggles again, "Yeah well, I only have one daddy and he's the strongest out of all the dads' in the family." I watch Alaric's chest puff up with pride.

THEIR FAMILY UNIT is very much like our own. I just wish they were here for the ceremony. I could reach out to them telepathically but I don't want to interrupt their missions. My brothers are busy as are my aunts and uncle.

"I am glad you will have someone here with you, Tia. Soon enough you will be surrounded by my entire family if you wish to stay here," I prompt to see if she wishes to keep my kingdom as her own or if I will become her consort.

"I would like to stay here but my title is firstborn, like yours. I wish to take over my throne after my mother," she tells me with a hint of nervousness.

I take a deep breath as if I were contemplating but knowing my answer will be to go with her to the Ice Kingdom. "Well, it looks like I'm leaving the nest, mother," I say loudly as I arch my back and arms stretching over my chair.

"I hear that Draven Kole Stormbringer," mother pipes in, "and you have our blessing."

Tia's excitement erupts as does my own. Suddenly her face drops as something crosses her mind.

"What's wrong, Tia?" I ask.

"I had a thought just now," she says peaking up at me from under her thick eyelashes. "I know you will have a hard time in the eternal winter as a frostless Dragon. If anything I will sacrifice for you and ask Ladon to ascend the throne," she tells me with confidence in her voice.

I hear a cough followed by a choking sound from over Tia's shoulder only to see Ladon hunched over trying to rid his throat of his draft.

"You okay over there, Ladon? I ask with laughter in my voice.

"I'll live, I think. Sissy, you've never told me you would give up your claim to the throne." He turns to face Tia fully and takes her hands in his. "Are you sure? That's something you might want to talk to mother and father about right now?" Ladon asks tentatively.

Tia looks up the table to Aurora and Alaric, her father is beaming with pride and her mother looks utterly confused. "No need for discussion baby brother. My mate holds title as do I, it's not as if I am taking a mate of a lower station than myself."

Tia stands and signals her brother to stand with her. As soon as he's standing she places her hand on his neck and pulls him down to touch her forehead to his. We can clearly hear her dragon crooning to his. "Ladon Uther Kraus, I Tiamat Andrea Kraus first in line give unto you all rights to ascend to the throne in the Ice Dragon court."

Frost spreads quickly over the two of them. For several moments they stand there holding onto each other tightly. Aurora is at the top of the table sniffling knowing how tough of a decision Tia just made. Ladon and Tia separate and Ladon kisses his sister's forehead before Tia returns to my side in silence.

"Ladon, I want to bestow a gift to you." I rise and move to his chair as we stand face to face. "My family is your family, my swarm is your swarm and my blood is your blood, this I swear." I shift a talon and slice my palm open and Ladon does the same.

"My family is your family, my swarm is your swarm and my blood is your blood. With my blood, this I swear,"

Ladon says as we clasp hands and the air around us becomes thick as our blood vows become concrete.

WE SMILE, nod our heads and we take our seats once more. This night keeps getting more and more interesting. I look to my mother and father who are tearing up with pride. I hear a sniffle closer to me and I see it's Tia.

"What's wrong, my love? What happened?" I asked slightly panicked.

"I am overcome with joy, Draven. This couldn't be a more joyous night! I am finally home," she states with tears and a smile.

I grab her hand and squeeze, attempting to assure her I am right here. Gently I use my thumb to wipe away her tears that became a little frosty on her cheeks. "We are home, here and with each other," I say.

"Now that the night has become quite interesting I think a dance is in order." Gently I kiss her cheek before rising slowly. "I need to speak with my mother quickly though to notify the family and my cousins. My grandfather and his mate will want to be here along with everyone else." Quickly I wrap Tiamat up in my arms and nuzzle her cheek. "Congratulations, my love, welcome to my family." Slowly I release her to be able to look her in the eyes.

Tia's eyes well up with unshed tears and her lip quivers. I feel her in my chest as I touch her scale and push back to her how much love I have for her. Unexpectedly Tia lunges for me and wraps her arms around my waist and buries her head under my chin. My heart explodes with joy knowing she sought me out for comfort and security. My eyes drift to Ladon and I catch him wiping away a tear before anyone spotted him doing it.

"Sorry to interrupt son, but I have reached out to the family and they will all be arriving for your ceremony. I know you will want them all present for this occasion." Mom tells me through our bond.

"Thank you, mother." I say happily.

"You okay, Draven?" Tia asks, as she nuzzles the underside of my jaw.

"Mother popped in my head to tell me my family will all be here tomorrow to celebrate our matching. What are the odds that all of them are done with vacation and their missions!" I say unable to contain my excitement. "Come on my love, let's go dance!"

I grab her hand and whisk her away to the open floor in the center of the room. Tia smiles as she looks up at me waiting for me to take hold of her for our first dance. Slowly she shakes her head at me and places one of my hands on her lower back. She's still giggling at me as she grips my left hand. Her left rests gently on my shoulder. Her eyes shift to her beast for a mere moment then back to normal. "Shall we begin my love?"

I give Tia a slight nod then look over to the orchestra and they begin a slow waltz. I lead her gently around the floor like we've done this a million times before. I can't believe how easy it is to move with her. I catch the glow around her eyes as the song changes, hesitantly she moves in closer to me and rests her head on the ball of my shoulder. I can finally hold her tightly to me. I enjoy feeling her warmth as well as the purr from her Dragoness. She's being extra cautious trying not to set either of us off giving us both this moment we so desperately needed.

"Is this okay? I can step back," Tia offers.

"No, please stay, don't move. I will hold you as long as you will allow me," I say, gently squeezing her. I hear her Dragoness purr a little louder so I release my hold to a little lighter. I don't want to push the envelope too far. Even if we don't have our sense of smell, I could accidentally trigger her and me both. A low rumble escapes my throat to answer her Dragoness and we find the harmony and love we have been looking for since we came of age.

"I can tell you are happy and spending time with you without wanting to maul each other sexually is nice," I say laughing.

"I am elated, Draven. Besides, I wouldn't know the first thing to do to sexually maul you." A soft giggle escapes her lips. "I'd be running on instinct and would follow you anywhere." She smiles innocently up at me.

"You may not know but your Dragoness will hunt me down if I don't give her what she wants once we have our sense of smell back. Are you ready to be mine?" I whisper close enough to her ear.

I can hear Tia breathe in deeply and hold her breath for a moment, I pull back a little bit and her eyes are closed. "I've been ready for the last twenty years." She opens her eyes and looks deeply into mine. I can see that she means every word she says.

"You mean to say you came of age at five?" I ask, shocked. She nods softly confirming my thoughts. "Tia, I came of age at eight. I've been waiting for you as long as you have for me." Gently I cup her cheeks looking into her eyes deeply. "I promise I will not let you down, we will honeymoon for a few weeks and I will show you everything you want," I say purring at her.

"*Draven!*" Ladon yells from across the room. Damn it.

"Even without your scent, you call to me on a primal level. I will make you *mine*," I growl at her, take her hand and lead her off the dance floor.

"You've turned her beet red, Draven! Nevermind, I don't want to know anymore," Ladon says exacerbated.

We both snicker at his dismay and take our seats to cool off and wait for dessert. Creme brulee is one of my number of favorites aside from cheesecake. The servants come by and place one in front of each of us. Tia and Ladon look at me as the topping is not crisped. I work my fire in my hand and blow it across their deserts and mine. Tia beams at me clapping her excitement while Ladon rolls his eyes at me.

After everything today, dinner, dessert, and the excitement tonight I could sleep for an entire day. Stretching back I rub my chest and stomach and see Tia eyeing my movements with her eyes turning mercury and back again. I appeal to her entirely and that makes me a lucky son of a bitch.

TWELVE

DRAVEN

"Walk with me, my love?" I ask Tia softly.

Tia looks to Ladon and he agrees that we can go alone without his supervision. We walk away from the festivities to the large balcony off to the side. It has a stunning view of the Stormbringer Kingdom and the smell of sea salt. I love flying but I love this moment even more.

"You look at peace, beloved," Tia says to me.

"I am because I know that you have been everything I have ever looked for. I won't dream and think that I am being haunted by an otherworldly being." I say wistfully. "You are that, but you are my world," I tell her, taking her hand again and kissing it. "Have I told you red is your color?"

"You haven't but I am sure you'll see my cheeks deepen in color if you continue your flattery," Tia tells me.

We look out into the night and see the moon casting light across the kingdom. The moon should be full tomorrow night and the Wolves in the north will be having their full moon celebration out in the woods. It's then I see a spec fly across the moon and motion to Tia for her to see as well.

Tia looks in the direction I pointed to and the spec that is in front of the moon. I watch her eyes shift to that of her Dragoness as she stares.

"It's Edgar and Odette! They're about thirty minutes out," Tia starts to bounce excitedly.

"*Ladon*! Odette is almost here, I can see Edgar!" I can see Tia fighting the urge to shift and fly out to meet her sister.

Gently I place my hand on Tia's back. "The wind is with them, my love. They will be here much faster than antici-pated." I smile trying to reassure her.

"I trust your judgement, beloved. Shall we return to the feast that's in our honor?" Tia says after searching the sky one last time.

"We will go back in once we greet your sister and Edgar. They need a welcoming committee, don't they?" I ask her being as playful as possible.

"Really? Oh, Draven, thank you!" she squeals a bit and takes off to the stairs of the castle.

I tail after her as does Ladon and our parents. The excite-ment I feel from Tia puts a broad smile on my face. She moves so gracefully, I can't help but eye her movements. Frost coats every step she takes leaving a trail a foot wide just like in my dreams. I scold myself knowing I have to rein it in but she makes it quite difficult not to get lost in her.

"*Odette!*" Tia squeals as her sister lands.

Odette slides off of Edgars back and runs straight for her sister. They squeal and hug and cry. I watch Ladon shaking his head looking at those two. "You never get used to them getting like that. You would think they were separated for months already," Ladon says laughing.

Tia drags Odette over to where I'm standing. Her smile is infectious and I can't help but smile back just as brightly. "Betrothed, this is Odette. Odette, this is my betrothed, Draven." Odette goes to step forward to greet me and Tia starts a deep threatening growl to the point the area's temperature instantly drops. She's possessive of me even with her sister.

Odette looks back to Tia and steps back and behind Tia and offers me a wave. "Nice to meet you Draven. I'll be honest, I've never seen Tia like this." She raises both eyebrows. "You're scary sis. You remind me of mom."

Tia is having a hard time reining in her possessiveness, I watch Ladon come over and lay a frost covered hand on Tia's neck. As her temperature drops she calms down.

"Sorry." Her eyes lock on Odette and she motions towards her. "...Unlike me.. Someone has gotten to experience life.." Tia bares her descended canines at Odette.

"I love you sissy, please don't go near Draven. We may have an accidental bear-cicle."

"Tia, you are welcome to stay by my side as you introduce Odette to my parents," I offer to dissolve some of the tension I feel from her.

Tia nods and steps away from her siblings, placing her hand in mine and gives me a throaty purr. This woman has no idea what she does to me even when she's not being possessive. I'll spontaneously combust if I don't watch it.

"Draven, you seem to have taken to my innocent sister quite quickly," Odette states plainly to me.

I look at Tia who is biting her tongue and I respond, "I am smitten with her personality, regardless of us being true mates. I cannot smell her and she cannot smell me so we are far better now than last night."

"Glad to hear that. I am happy for you both!" Odette says as she places her arm in Ladon's and we make our way back up to the entrance.

"Odette, how wonderful to see you!" My mom says as she embraces Odette quickly with a peck to each cheek.

"We haven't seen you in so long, you have grown up fast." my father says, nodding to her.

Odette nods and heads to her parents, embracing them. Edgar is behind Ladon and the crew, we make eye contact and nod. I wonder what Edgar is to the family? I don't remember Ladon talking about him.

"Let's all head in to continue our celebration!" Tia announces. She gives my hand a squeeze and we go back in.

THE FESTIVITIES ARE in full swing with everyone dancing, drinking and eating. This is what our kingdom needs, unity and relaxation. Tia pulls away from my hand hesitantly and goes to show Odette the ice sculpture I did for her. A servant comes by and hands Ladon and I a mug of dark beer each. We clink our glasses and sit back watching everyone mingle.

"Ladon, who is Edgar to the Ice Kingdom?" I curiously ask.

"Edgar, Dante and Marco were my grandmother Anca's guards. When my grandfather Nicodeamus was rescued by my mother he started searching for them." Ladon motions to Alaric.

"Just so happens the trio were in my father's court still serving the Ice Dragon Throne." Ladon starts to laugh. "Those poor guys draw straws as to who is going to watch over my mother. She's a bit of a handful when she's angry."

Ladon looks affectionately over at Tia. "The guys tend to fight over who gets to watch Tia. Up until now she was the easier one to watch over." He raises his eyebrows looking at me. "I wonder why? Hmmm.."

"I can only imagine, brother. Just keep in mind you are the one who connected the dots," I state, clinking my mug with his. "Now she is mine and my families to protect and save from herself. I know it will calm down after tomorrow."

"And I will be far far away from your honeymoon spot!" Ladon exclaims.

I spit out my beer a bit but recover quickly. "Thanks, I don't want to give you nightmares," I say laughing. I only get an eye roll from him.

"Speaking of...where are you taking my twin?" Ladon inquires.

"It's to be a surprise but I will tell you only because I know you fret about her otherwise." I take a deep breath and explain my plans. "I want to take her to Alaska, I figure it's summer there and parts are still frozen." I shrug slightly. "We can hit the Winter Palace and the Summer Chalet on our way back here." I'm trying to be as thoughtful as possible.

"Will you be going by plane or flying together?" asks Ladon.

"I will ask her if she wishes to ride on my Drake to get there. I don't want her to be exhausted when we arrive," I say plainly.

"Brother, there were too many innuendos in that!" Ladon all but yells at me.

"I did *not* mean it that way! I was serious for once." I say all joking aside. Deep in my heart I just want to do everything that will make my mate happy and comfortable.

"She will want to fly or ride not go by plane," says Ladon.

"Good. Then it's settled. You can tell everyone where we went once we are gone. I don't want any interruptions." Slowly I raise my mug and take a deep drink of it.

"Speaking of interruptions, I see someone I would like to dance with this evening. IF you don't mind, here--hold my beer," Ladon says handing his mug to me.

I STIFLE a laugh and look for my woman and her sister. They are at the table chatting away, catching up. Tia leans forward and Odette whispers something in her ear that turns her face a brilliant crimson. Tia's eyebrows shoot straight up and her mouth pops open making a perfect "O".

Odette nods profusely and Tia dives back in to listen to more of what Odette has to say. I can feel a fear and anxiety roll through Tia like a freight train. The frost coats the area around Tia showing her distress. I'm curious about their discussion, but I don't wish to interrupt.

Casually I stroll over to Alaric. "M'lord." I bow slightly and he to me in return.

"Please, call me Dad. After tomorrow we will be family and both kingdoms will have an even stronger alliance." Alaric rests his hand on my shoulder and gives it a squeeze.

"Thanks Dad, I was wondering if it was inappropriate to call you father yet," I chuckle softly then motion with my beer stein to Tia and Odette. "I'm almost frightened about what they are talking about. The mixed feelings coming off of Tia is making my head spin," I state plainly.

"Oh son, I'm sure Odette is giving her a lot to think about. Besides, her birth father believed in allowing her to experience the world entirely if you catch my drift." Alaric raises his eyebrows and I just nod agreeing.

"I'll be honest, Draven, part of me wishes I had let Tia date some." He sighs and runs his hand over his face.

"On the flip side, I'm glad I did refrain from allowing her to date. What if she forced a bond on someone to not be alone?" He sighs and stares down at his beer for a moment then looks back up at me. "She's strong enough to do it. God's know she terrifies me when she gets mad." Alaric looks around to see where Aurora is.

"I'd rather deal with her mother in a rage than Tia." Alaric looks around again expecting Aurora to pop up at any moment. "She's mastered permafrost! I can't throw permafrost. Her Dragoness is a throw back to her great-great grandmother the Blood Queen. Huge, powerful and immune to just about everything," He shakes his head then smirks looking at me. "Good luck son...," Alaric turns and leaves to go find his mate.

I've learned more about Tia, and I couldn't be more proud to have her as my mate. The concerning piece is her missing her family. If she was away for only a few days I can't imagine how she'll be when she's here permanently. I steady myself and head over to a terrified Tia.

"Odette...are you giving Tia terrifying images?" I ask her coyly.

"Never dear brother to be, I was merely explaining how this really works to my sister. There is no harm in that," she says with a bright smile.

"Tia, would you like a breather and relax?" I ask.

Tia slowly stands and offers me her hand. "Can you find me a glass of red wine beloved? I feel like my poor head is spinning from such imagery." She smiles at me as we walk towards the balcony.

"Anything you want, my love." I motion to one of the servers and ask him for red wine and another beer for myself.

I TAKE our drinks out to the balcony and meet a distressed Tia there. I don't say a word as I walk up beside her and hand her the glass. I place my elbows on the rail as I wait for her to gather herself and speak to me.

"Is it truly as horrifying as my sister makes it out to be for a woman's first time?" she asks.

"I am sure your sister exaggerated substantially. I promise I'll take care of you," I say to her with my voice full of emotion.

Gently I caress her cheek trying to bring her some semblance of comfort.. I know that all of this must be scary but at the same time I know she is strong like her mother. The battle on the field showed me just that along with her reaction being territorial over me when her sister arrived.

"I can tell that you were scared, my love. Deep in my heart I know that everything will be alright as long as we are together.." Gently I kiss her cheek and hug her to me. "I trust you and your Dragoness that no harm will come to me." I laugh softly trying to lighten the mood.

"Thank you, betrothed. I know I should have more confidence in my Dragoness and I do, but I do not have confidence in myself as a woman," she says taking a deep breath. "As inexperienced as I am, I can't help but be slightly nervous," she tells me. "What if I do hurt you? What if she does get out of control?" Tia moves away pacing back and forth, she's a ball of nervous energy.

Tia stops short and spins to look at me. "What if? What if you, how did Odette put it; Horde the chicken.. No horde the cock and my Dragoness gets angry?" Tia tilts her head looking at me quite seriously.

Suddenly, I inhale my saliva down the wrong pipe and

start coughing profusely. Did she really tell her that that's what it is called? After a few rounds of clearing my throat do I finally find my voice.

"Well, I guess that's one way of saying it." I can't help but laugh a little. "I can assure you I will never hide any of my body parts from you," I tell her with laughter in my voice. "I can also promise you that after our first night, I don't think that I could hide from your Dragoness if I wanted to."

I watch in wonder as her eyes turn mercury and back again. I'm sure my dragon eyes flickered for her as well.

"Alright love birds," Alaric says. "We are about to start the last dance of the evening, the renaissance dance.

Tia smiles sweetly and lowers her head to Alaric. "Thank you Daddy!" Tia gently lays a hand on my cheek then looks back to her father. "Do you mind if I dance with my father?"

Gently I take her hand in mine and kiss her knuckles. "If that's what your heart desires then please do so. I'll go speak with my parents and make sure everything is in order for tomorrow."

Tia smiles and lowers her head slightly to me before moving to her father. She places her hand on his forearm and follows him out onto the dance floor. I watch them move slowly and gracefully across the floor. Two apex deadly predators make this dance look effortless.

My eyes are locked on my beautiful mate enjoying this dance with her father. Whatever he's saying to her has her laughing hysterically. He does a graceful lift and spin with her and she looks like an angel that's come down to earth.

Next thing I know Ladon punches my shoulder. "Earth to Draven. Dude! I've been calling your name for like five minutes. You ok man? Your mom sent me to get you." He smirks, this can't be good.

"I was entranced by your father and Tia's relationship, they are really close," I say quietly. I inhale deeply and walk with Ladon to my mom to talk about the ceremony.

"Hello, mother." I say on a sigh sneaking a peek at my mate.

"Hi Draven, have you been enjoying your evening?" she asks with a sly smile.

"I have certainly enjoyed the evening so far. I am ready for tomorrow!" I tell her with enthusiasm.

"Well, we do need to discuss a few things about tomorrow," she says as an itinerary forms before her and she goes to check her list. "I want to make sure we have everyone in attendance and the decorations perfect," she goes on and I tilt my head so she knows I am listening. "I have the entryway lined up, the walkway with different height candles with your red flames. There are also the ice flowers down the aisle way, draped with dangling ice roses. Is there anything else you would like me to add?"

"I'm honestly not sure Mom. I'm sure whatever you and Aurora come up with for us will be perfect." I smile and look back at my mate again before refocusing on my mother. "I just want tomorrow to be a dream come true for Tia like it is for me."

"The first of many, son. Now, I think we have everything together for tomorrow. The last thing to do is to get some rest and finish out our tournament tomorrow so we can match you two tomorrow night!" she says excitedly. "Go find your lady love and I will let you know when the family arrives in the morning. They are coming from all over the United States and South America. I can't wait to have everybody back together!"

"I am excited that they will all be here for my mating ceremony and meet Tia. I think everybody will love her and also want to see her Dragoness," I say with a chuckle.

Mother grabs my beard and pulls it lovingly, telling me that our conversation has come to an end. I kiss her on the cheek and walk off to find my woman.

TIA IS BACK out on the balcony with all of the people trying to get close and touch her is making her uncomfortable. Ladon is standing beside Tia as well as Odette. "I don't believe in letting others touch me! I am betrothed! Do you not get it Odette?" Tia has her back to the ballroom and frost is coating the balcony. Scales can be seen rippling up and down her arms to her hands.

"Chill sis! It's no big deal!" She raises her hands then drops them." Weren't you the one always complaining that you wish you were as free as me. The man wanted a dance that is all. No big deal." Odette shrugs her shoulders not seeing why her sister is so worked up.

Tia's Dragoness practically roars at Odette. "I will not be touched by anyone other than my mate!" Ice and frost bursts out in all directions from Tia as she stares down her sister who's eyes have blackened to that of her Bear.

I roar out in rage and allow my fire and lighting to encase my body but not fully shift. I push my way through to get to my mate and protect her, even from her sister.

"Odette, I will warn you now to abide by your sister's wishes or you will sit the night in the dungeon," I threaten her, my voice is thick with my dragon so close to the surface.

"I don't mean any harm I just don't understand what the big deal is!" Odette says to me.

"I don't want anyone else to touch me, only Draven! I've dreamt of him for *years*, and he has about me as well." Tia bares her canines at her sister as frost escapes her lips. "I don't want to be some whore and not cherish what gift I have been given!" Tia yells at Odette.

Alaric comes out onto the balcony with his arms shifted to his gauntlets ready to go to war if need be. He sees how distressed his birth daughter and bond daughter are. His eyes next fall on me and my flames then back to Tia. "Baby girl what's happened?"

Tia's eyes are that of her Dragoness, their liquid mercury swirls almost blotting out her black slits. "My sister doesn't understand that I will not allow another male to touch me in any way shape or form." Tia practically growls out her words, her canines fully visible while she speaks.

"Is that true Odette?" Alaric calms down slightly and shifts his arms back to normal.

"It's no big deal father, the nice man just wanted to dance with her. Tia refused. She's always crying about isolation, not being hugged enough. Blah blah blah..." At the last blah out of her mouth a thick sheet of ice covers her lips and Aurora is standing there tapping her foot.

"You're being sent home, Odette. Your birth father can deal with your insolence." Aurora growls out. "Tia is not like you! She has dreamed of her mate since she was five years old!" The bone plates in Aurora's face visibly move. "Do you not understand the amount of heartache this poor girl has endured?" Aurora growls. "I don't blame Tia for wanting to avoid everyone," Aurora snorts frost in her daughter's direction. "Edgar is waiting for you out front. Go home." Aurora ushers Odette out of sight.

I simmer down, letting my flames and lighting die out. I walk up to Tia with slight hesitancy knowing that I could potentially set her off. I stand a foot away from her as Ladon gives us some space. After about five minutes Tia regains her composure and rushes forward wrapping her arms around my waist.

"No one will *ever* touch me but you," she says quietly.

"I won't stand for it. You. Are. *Mine*," I say with my beast in my throat. I am protective of her and she will know it.

"I must say I am quite happy to see how you protected me, even against my own sister. She deserved your anger and my families. Papa Bear will take care of her and set her straight," she tells me with a sigh.

"I am glad that didn't get any worse. I have never in my life seen you blow your lid like that, Draven. You look like you were about to assassinate Odette!" Ladon says with a little humor.

"The thought did cross my mind." I say raising my eyebrows.

Tia playfully hits my arm and Ladon's. "Now I have to find someone else to stand with me tomorrow."

"Tia, what about Luna?" Aurora raises her eyebrows looking at Tia waiting to see if her suggestions would be acceptable.

"Perfect mother! Please have Marco or Dante bring her tomorrow." Tia smiles broadly then looks at me. "You have to promise to turn down the Alpha around Luna." Tia's puppy eyes make my heart melt. "My baby sister is an Omega and easily frightened."

"Anything you desire, love it's yours. I'll do my best to turn down the Alpha." I wink at Tia making her blush.

"It's settled then. Dante will arrive with Luna in the morning." Aurora says as she turns to leave.

"If you'll excuse me, I need to go talk to our mothers' about what's appropriate for me to wear tomorrow." Tia gently caresses my cheek before motioning to her father to escort her off.

"Wow, besides you getting all murdery, seeing Tia just about rip her second favorite sister apart was shocking." Ladon says rubbing the back of his neck. "I do have to say that Odette was right though. All Tia has ever wanted was to be touched and held." Ladon shrugs his shoulders. "I can kinda see where the misunderstanding is since Odette has never been here." Ladon puts his hands up in a placating manner. "I'm not saying that she was right to try and force contact against Tia's will."

"I also can understand where her sister is coming from. Unfortunately tonight was not the night to have such a conversation, or try to push somebody into dancing with my mate of all people," I say exhaling a deep breath.

"WHERE IS that little weasel Odette tried getting Tia to dance with?" We both scan the area looking for the guy. It's funny how you know when someone is in trouble by the way that they constantly shift their eyes around looking for any danger. My eyes finally land on one male in particular who is drinking and chatting away with women surrounding him. I can't quite put my finger on it but something feels off.

I tap Ladon on the shoulder getting his attention and toss my head to the side showing him that I have located the man. We both move in stealth fashion around the dining hall and pop up on either side of him unbeknownst to him. The women scurry away and the man turns around to stare at us both in shock.

"So I hear my mate is of interest to you. What kind of an insult is this?" My eyes shift to that of my dragon. "Are you unable to face me?" I prod at the male.

"Prince Draven, I...I knew better but she drew me in with her scent," he says cautiously.

"Excuse the *fuck* out of me? *You scented my mate?*" I roar out with my scales erupting over my body. Tendrils of lightning pulsing through my hair.

"I think now is a good time to run dude. You know he'll shred you." Ladon narrows his eyes at the weasel. "Consider this a warning, don't ever go after my sister, his mate, *ever* again," Ladon says coldly as scales ripple over his exposed arms.

"I, I'm so sorry, your highness!" the male says.

Ladon places his hand on my shoulder sending a cold chill through my body to get me to calm down. I take a few deep breath's in and out attempting to relax.

"Draven, son, is everything okay?" Mom says through our bond.

"It is now, mother. I almost lost my cool on that imbecile."
I replied quickly to her.

"I am proud of you for keeping your cool. Your show of restraint is impressive." She takes a dramatic pause. *"Now, when you see your mate tomorrow that may be a different story..."* My mother says softly warning me of my increased protective drive.

"Are you good, brother?" Ladon asks.

"I am good now. My mom just popped in my head to check in on me." Smirking I shrug my shoulders. "She says I may not be able to restrain myself very well tomorrow as I did just now," I tell him.

"This better be one fast ceremony or all of us are in trouble I believe." he says with a slight chuckle.

I shake my head holding back my laugh then take a few jabs at his torso. We horse around for a few moments then take off for more drinks. With our metabolism we burn it off so fast it would take an eighteen wheeler full to get me drunk.

IN THE DISTANCE I catch sight of a crowd gathering over where my parents are seated. As Ladon and I approach we can see Tia and her mother both with their arms shifted to their gauntlets. "Shhhh.. watch this.. they don't do this too often." Ladon whispers to me.

Tia and Aurora rub their talons together causing an arch

of what looks like lightning between them. They hold their hands out towards each other and frost begins to gather. Both sets of eyes have an ethereal glow to them as they concentrate on the power.

An object begins to form in the center between them. As it takes form we can make out an ice sculpture of my parents' dragons' in flight. The sculpture seems to look alive as a spark of energy pulses in the hearts of the dragons.

Carefully Tia and Aurora grip the sculpture and sit it before my mother. The joy this gift has brought her is immense. Gisella jumps up and hugs Aurora and Tia, thanking them profusely. Tia draws in a deep breath and shifts her hands back. Tia blushes a beautiful shade of pink having noticed the crowd around her. Quickly she moves and snuggles up to her father as others attempt to approach her.

"Give the royals some space please," I bellow out getting upset with seeing Tia nervous.

Everyone takes a good six steps back from the area as I approach. My eyes must be that of my Dragon since everyone is avoiding eye contact and looking at the ground. Gently I take the sculpture and place it on the table closest to the serving area so it may be displayed for everyone to see and take the attention away from my woman. I walk back over to her and open my arms for her to snuggle against me. She may be her father's daughter but she is mine now as well.

Tia gently kisses her father's cheek then comes over to me quickly without hesitation. "Your dragon is showing," she says as she smiles looking up at me.

I can't help but laugh a little. "I saw how uncomfortable you were with everyone around you. I got a little defensive."

"I love how possessive you are of me," she says bashfully as she places a gentle kiss under my chin.

We stay like this for sometime until our evening comes to a close and we must rest for the day to come. I'm tempted beyond reason to kiss her thoroughly but bite my bottom lip instead.

"What are you thinking, my beloved?" Tia asks me.

"Just thinking about how badly I want to kiss you," I say in a low growl.

Tia turns slightly and stares at me directly with her eyes bleeding over to her liquid mercury. I don't know how she does it but every time her eyes shift I become entranced with her.

"You are sinful, Mr. Stormbringer," she scolds me.

"Only for you, Mrs. Stormbringer," I tell her.

I place my hand under her chin tilting her head up towards me slightly as my thumb and forefinger caress her jaw line. She shivers visibly and before I know it a burst of wind pushes the two of us apart.

"Draven...," my mother scolds, "behave son."

Tia and I both start laughing and Ladon hits me upside the head. I swear I don't know what I'm doing half the time when it comes to her. I might want to go take a cold shower immediately. Tia turns three shades of pink looking between my mother and her brother.

"TIA, you're staying with me tonight." Ladon takes Tia by the hand and leads her to the wing their parents are in. Oddly enough he leads her out into the courtyard. "One last time big sis?" Tia nods once then looks back to my mother and I.

I look at my best friend as he shifts to that of his Dragon. "Good night beloved. Good night Mom." Tia smiles as she turns and starts walking towards Ladon.

Tia's shift is much slower than Ladon's and there's definitely a lot more frost involved. Her Dragoness dwarfs her brothers, carefully they wrap their bodies together. Each dragon hides their head under the other's wing to sleep.

A layer of frost and ice covers their bodies encasing them together. "Why did they do that?" I question.

Alaric steps out of the shadows and lays a hand on my shoulder. "You don't get it do you?" Alaric smiles and chuckles softly.

"They were born under the Dragon Moon with the Dragon Star at its apex." He motions to the stars above.

"They are yin and yang. In essence they complete the other, and bring balance." Alaric looks his two children over.

"Twins are rare with Ice Dragons, females are even more rare. I was blessed with twins and a daughter." Alaric reminisces.

"Tia made herself known and hid her brother the entire pregnancy. She still protects him even now." Alaric smiles wistfully looking at his sleeping children. "His edge in battle, that's her boosting his power." Alaric smiles before he touches the ice. "They'll wake up with the sun in the morning. I'll have breakfast waiting for them." Alaric turns and addresses the gathered family. "Everyone is welcome to join us." Alaric says before disappearing again.

The people in attendance look at the two in astonishment. They've never seen much outside of the other supernaturals in our community. We have a Hotel Darkfang to the north that houses our international and inter-species guests, but never has anyone seen dragons like Tia and Ladon. Alaric is right, he is blessed—in more ways than he knows.

THIRTEEN

TIAMAT

THE SUN BREAKS OVER THE HORIZON PAINTING THE sky like an artist's canvas. The first rays of light begin creeping over the hedges in the garden. The breakfast spread is set at the table that Alaric arranged for the morning. Both families wait anxiously for us to awaken. The most on edge is my mother. I can feel her, she's prowling the courtyard as her hybrid beast. The occasional whine can be heard as she tests the ice prison we are sleeping in.

The rays of the sun finally start touching us slowly melting the ice. No one moves or makes a sound watching in wonder. My rumble is the first sound heard from the icy mass, second is the initial cracking of the ice.

Rapidly the ice begins to melt and the sound of my ignitor click is heard. I am the first of the twins to wake up and I'm on edge. Mother stands at the ready, clicking her talons in anticipation of a possible battle.

I raise my head suddenly ready to freeze the first being that comes near my brother. My lips pull back over my teeth just as I'm getting ready to rain frost flames upon my enemy. My mother's Lycan beast leaps up and I catch her in my taloned hand. *Not today mother.. not today..*

I lick my mother's beast then set her down before nudging my brother to wake him up. Ladon slowly wakes up and shakes his head getting rid of the last of the ice. I lower my great horned head and nuzzle Ladon encouraging him to get up again. Carefully I lift my wing out of the way for him to move.

Ladon looks back to me and warns me he's about to shift and hide my face. I turn my head back toward my body and hide it under my wing.

"Baby girl, you can come out now." I hear my father call to me.

Slowly I lift my wing and bring my head back out to look at everyone assembled. Trusting in Gisella's mages magic I shift back to my human form. It's always such a slow and uncomfortable process for me because of my Dragoness' size. I breathe in a deep breath and stretch. "Forgive my appearance, I didn't get the chance to change before bed." I say softly.

Three short barks sound and I turn to face my mother's beast. *"Tia, I have a gift for you. Come closer."*

I move to my mother swiftly and look up into her beasts eyes. Her taloned hands grip my head tightly. *"This is going to hurt, I'm sorry my hatchling."*

Mother's words barely register before I feel like my insides are being boiled from the inside. A foreign power rips through my body. I scream out in pain and scales ripple over my flesh. I feel my mates panic, I'd hate to know what this looks like to him.

Eventually mom releases me and I fall to my knees panting heavily. I feel different, my Dragoness feels stronger. She's admiring her scales in my mind saying our armor is stronger.

Mother finally comes over to me wearing a robe. "I'm sorry I hurt you my hatchling." Mom kisses my cheeks. "I shared with you the power of the ancient Gallus. It's my wedding gift to you." Mom kisses my forehead then walks to dad.

"*Tiamat!*" Draven yells as he runs to my side. "What the hell just happened?" he asks, checking me over and shooting my mother a look. "Someone explain, please."

"I have gifted my daughter an added weapon of defense, my son to be. She is much stronger now and her Dragoness seems quite pleased," Aurora tells me.

"It's true, betrothed—it is a great gift indeed!" I say beaming at him.

"A mating gift, that is very kind of you mother," Draven tells my mom. "Well, we've had a very festive morning indeed! My love, might I do your hair for you?" Draven offers.

I step away and give him a shy smile with a nod. I feel him tugging and pulling gently at my long light blonde locks. Almost a half hour later he completes his task and he takes a picture with his phone to show me. I absolutely love what he's done to my hair.

"Hatchling...you look like a Viking Queen." Mother tells me. "You are a surprise, Draven. Tia is quite lucky to have you, as are we."

I blush profusely as I run my hands over my hair. It feels as beautiful as it looks, seems that my mate has many surprises up his sleeves. Draven looks quite pleased with his work.

"Thank you, mother. I will do anything for her. Now let's go eat, I am famished as I am sure you are all as well," he says then takes my hand and places it in his elbow.

"I could eat a stag right now." I laugh softly then look up at him. The stag being our inside joke. Ladon almost chokes on his juice and everyone looks at him oddly.

"Tiamat, I have placed a gown in your room that Oberon had made special for you for this day." My mom says gently.

Draven watches my eyes light up at the thought of a fae crafted gown waiting for me. "Truly mother?" My eyebrows shoot up in shock. "He went through the trouble of having it made? I am no one special." I say with confusion in my voice.

"No one special? You are my granddaughter, you are the most precious." Nicodeamus stands in the doorway looking at his gathered family. Slowly he opens his arm and I run to him.

"You came!" I say, crying tears of joy holding onto my grandfather.

It's been years since Draven last saw him. "Thank you for coming on such short notice, sir." Draven says bowing graciously to Nicodeamus.

"The pleasure is all mine son." Nicodeamus releases me and starts to walk around Draven as if examining him. "I can tell a great warrior when I see one. I believe you are a good match for my Tia." Nicodeamus offers Draven his hand to shake.

"Thank you m'lord, that means a great deal coming from you," Draven says, taking Nicodeamus's hand. "I am happy to have surprised Tia. And your presence here helps boost our kingdom's knowledge knowing that we are unified," he says releasing Nicodeamus's hand.

"We have had an eventful morning thus far," Queen Gisella states. "Let us prepare for our day with a full stomach and enjoy each other's company before the tournament begins," she says holding her arm open towards the dining hall for us to all enter.

It's at that moment my stomach growls and Draven laughs at me. "Hungry this morning, my love?"

"Famished," I say.

Draven takes me to our table and pulls out my chair for me to have a seat. He winks at me and takes off to the kitchen. I find myself wondering what he is up to but grandfather catches my attention pulling me into a conversation.

"Tiamat, tell me, you seem to be taken with this young man. Is your heart happy?" Grandfather asks me.

"My heart is full, grandfather. I believe to explain better that what I feel...is how you feel for Helle," I respond.

Nicodeamus's face splits into a wide smile at my commentary. All he does is mutter "good, good" and goes back to drinking his tea. The one thing I want in life is to have a strong dependable and faithful mate for the rest of my unnatural life and I am glad that I have just that.

"Your breakfast is served, my love," Draven announces as he places my plate before me.

My eyes go wide at what he has presented to me. There is a large plate of raw meat including fresh tuna and venison. I hear my stomach growl once again; my mate knows me so well already.

"Thank you, betrothed!" I tell him excitedly. I glance over at Draven as he sits with his own plate of raw meats and begins to light them on fire ever so slightly. "Did you hunt these yourself, betrothed?"

"Indeed I did, I wanted you to eat well this morning and I understand you like your meat rare or raw. Am I correct?" he asks me and tilts his head to the side.

I smile affectionately at my mom. "Mother taught us to hunt and survive off of the land and sea. It's harder to hide poison in raw meat than cooked." I blush slightly. "I appreciate that you hunted for me. You'll be a good provider when the time comes that I am with hatchling."

Ladon spits his drink and starts coughing trying to clear his lungs. Alaric quickly starts hitting his sons back trying to help him clear his lungs.

"One day my love, maybe not just yet though," He says tentatively with a small smile.

I think I made the man blush, but why? Oh well, I would rather be devouring this dish. Chatter begins around us all as Draven's people stop by the table to wish him and Ladon well in the aerial fight today. This will be my favorite part of the tournament yet. I wish I could fight in it as well as the boys but I know mother would have my hide.

"TIA, would you like to walk the grounds with me and be with me while I get ready for my flight?" Draven asks quietly near my ear.

I nod my head and the two of us excuse ourselves. Ladon is right behind us, close as usual to make sure we don't do anything stupid. I am always the one protecting him and here he is protecting the two closest people to him.

"Ladon, you might want to walk away from this conversation, brother," Draven says.

"Say no more," he says, throwing his hands in the air. "I'll be near but not too close."

"He's so dramatic lately," Draven says laughing. "Now, where were we."

Draven pushes me up against the tent with his hands on my upper arms. My Dragoness rises to the surface enjoying his actions. I am glad I don't have my sense of smell or this could get bad for us both.

"I will give you as many hatchlings as you want, Tia. I promise you that," he tells me in a gruff voice that sends chills throughout my body and to my lower abdomen.

"I would like that, very much," I tell him without reservation.

I'm greeted with his response of his pelvis leaning into me and I feel his hard shaft pressed against me. I think Odette is right, my Dragoness won't be denied as I growl and my lip curls. I want this man in ways I don't even know yet. I will gladly let him lead until I figure it all out and turn the tables.

"My little Dragoness likes what she feels, yes?" Draven taunts me.

"We both do," I tell him with my tongue peaking out to lick my lips.

"You respond so well to me, I cannot wait until tonight," he says.

"*Alright* you two, break it up! I can smell you both from the downdraft two miles away!" Ladon yells. "We have a tournament to prepare for."

"I know what I want to prepare," I say as Draven backs up giving me space, "a little brother icicle!" I say throwing frost at his balls.

Draven laughs and tosses a small flame at Ladon to thaw him. We all get a good chuckle and move on to their tent. The boys get ready by stretching and sparring slightly with each other. One day I would like to spar with Draven myself, I know he is an assassin but I am lethal in my own right.

"Brother, would you be upset if I were to enter the tournament for today only?" I inquire.

"I will not allow it," Draven chimes in. "Any other time would be fine but not the day of our ceremony, please, my love."

"I am with Draven, sister," he states dryly.

"If you need a stress relea...," Draven starts to say but gets interrupted by Ladon punching him in the jaw.

"Don't finish that sentence, I can't hear these things," Ladon complains.

Ladon barely finishes his sentence before I'm partially shifted and have him up in the air by his throat. My scales ripple up and down my body as I growl at him. "How dare you hit my mate."

I can feel the power radiating from me, the new essence mother gave me increasing my strength even in this lithe form. I feel my canines descend as I bare them at my brother. I feel as if I am going insane, I want to rip him apart for hurting my mate.

"Tia, calm down baby, look I am okay. There is no blood spilled and I am in one piece." Draven tries to get my attention. *"Take a deep breath then exhale, focus on my voice. Let it soothe over you like a calm rain."* Draven says, trying to reassure me through our bond.

I focus on his voice in my head and take a deep breath that is needed so I do not injure my own blood. *What just happened to me?* I shake my head trying to clear it. I release Ladon and feel the shame rolling off me in waves. "Brother, I...I am sorry but I saw you hit my mate and I could only see red. Forgive me," I say, lowering my head feeling guilty.

Ladon sighs and nods before moving in to hug me. "It's ok sissy, it's almost over." He kisses my temple and his Dragon tries to croon to mine. I feel horrible that I wanted to hurt my brother over what would be normal for them. *What's wrong with me?*

"You're too good to me baby brother." I force a smile and attempt to laugh. "I'm supposed to protect you, and yet I hurt you again. I feel like the worst sister in the world." Several tears roll down my cheeks. "I don't know what's wrong with me. I feel at war with myself." I rest my fore-head on his shoulder.

"You will feel whole after tonight. Don't fret sissy, all will be well." Ladon kisses my forehead. "Why don't you two spar for a few moments? Nothing major, only jabs and defensive passes. You need to blow off some steam." He smiles at me as he backs away.

"You attack and I'll defend. Come on let's have it," Draven says assuming the defensive stance. I look at him like he's gone mad but he's brilliant. It's just what I need for the time being.

Nodding slowly I go to the table and find the wrappings there and have Ladon help me wrap my forearms and fists. Out of the corner of my eye I watch Draven wrap his fists up as well. Ladon helps me stretch and get ready for the sparring match.

I watch Draven stretch and my mouth waters seeing his muscles ripple. I'm hypnotized watching the expansion and contraction of his muscles. Ladon taps my shoulder getting my attention and snapping me out of my daze.

Slowly I approach Draven sizing him up, he's in a stance that says he's more right side dominant. He jabs lightly testing his reach, quickly I slap his hand away. He smirks looking at me then comes up quick with his left. Grabbing his wrist I use his momentum against him and throw him off balance. Instead he sees what I'm trying to do and tries to toss me instead.

Laughing I don't let go and take him with me and trip

him up. I fake my move to strike his knee and take his feet out from under him. As he lands on his back I sit on his chest with my talons at his throat.

"Got you," I say with a smile on my face. Slowly I bend down and kiss him on the tip of his nose.

"You will always have me," he tells me.

"You mean to tell me you let me win?" I say with sadness.

"No, my love, I mean I will never harm you. You won that on your own." He smiles brightly. "You are quite fast and absolutely mesmerizing," he says with admiration in his voice. I help him off the floor and let the boys resume their ways of prepping for battle.

FOURTEEN

LADON

THE TIME HAS COME FOR ME TO SHINE. PART OF ME wishes my sister could join in this battle and the other part wants to keep her safe. Draven does me the solid favor of locking my clothing with my shift so I don't have to worry about flashing my junk. I wait in the tunnel for my name to be called.

Tia is updating me how the other matches are going and by the looks of it, she's updating Draven as well. It makes me wonder exactly how deep their connection is without completing the bond. I sigh softly, for once I'm jealous of Tia. Jealous that the Princess that was almost literally locked in a tower found her mate.

I shake my head slowly trying to refocus on the task at hand. Slowly I roll my neck and stretch my limbs out of habit. My Dragon is chomping at the bit wanting to display his power. Maybe, just maybe my mate will be watching. Maybe she's in the stands or arriving today for the ceremony. One can hope, right?

I hear my name announced and I stride confidently out into the arena. It appears I will be facing off against Tyron, an Earth Dragon. From what I know they are large and slow, I'm not exactly sure how his breath weapon will work in the air.

The announcement for us to shift sounds and my dragon rips free. I lift my head and roar as loudly as I can. Ice shoots out in all directions under my feet as I walk. Tyron looks at me concerned before taking to the air.

I bolt after him chasing through the aerial obstacle course. I somehow lose him after a turn, then get blasted on my underbelly by rocks. *Crap!* That's how it's going down. I have to be in his line of sight for him to aim at me.

Tia warns me where he is so I start to hunt him again. Tyron panics as I start using my breath weapon on him. I catch him going around a corner and freeze his wing solid. He falls from the sky like a stone. Quickly I dive and grab his wings with my taloned hands. I slow his descent back to earth and help him land safely.

I land not too far away and roar triumphantly. My name resounds throughout the arena and the crowd goes wild. I look up towards Tia in the royal box. She smiles and waves at me, and I can feel the pride she has over my performance. I shift back quickly and wave to the crowd as I walk back into the tunnel.

"YOU'RE NEXT BROTHER!" I clap Draven on the back.

"This ought to be fun," he says with a mischievous smirk.

Draven is paired with a Blue Dragon named Eagan. He is weaker than Draven and in a lot of senses so I wonder how he made it this far. The only reason he may have made it is due to his dragon fire shield of a hide. They are a coveted mate to have as well as a battle partner in your corner.

Draven and Eagan takeoff into the sky and they shift forms, both throwing blasts of fire at each other. Draven is not being hurt but he is attacking Eagan as well but without damage. Draven has to outsmart him in order to take him down to the ground. I watch them closely with my eyes shifted to keep up. Draven flies backward into large circles going up underneath Eagan grabbing his talons with a hiss.

With a huge burst, Draven flaps his wings backward dragging Eagan down to the ground. Unfortunately, Eagan recovers due to his smaller size as a Blue Dragon. Draven roars out angrily then dives for Eagan, both of their fire flames hit each other at the exact same moment. I must say Eagan is talented but Draven is better.

Draven dodges out of the way breaking their fire contact. The man is sneaky and uses his lighting attack and shocks the hell out of Eagan. He's stunned just long enough for Draven to get the upper hand and drive Eagan to the ground. The crowd goes absolutely insane with cheers. Draven shifts back into his human form fully clothed with his arms raised high in the air in victory.

TIA THROWS a massive blast of ice in the air and Queen Gisella uses her lighting to shred it into twinkling snowflakes. They rain down around us, dusting the grounds, and yet they still shimmer, what a sight to behold.

"Quiet everyone, quiet please!" Queen Gisella announces with her voice magnified. "The battles have been weighed and measured by the crowd. It seems as though we have our champion for this season. Prince Draven Stormbringer!" she yells.

Another round of cheers erupts and magical fireworks blow up in the sky above. Looking at the display it shows many Dragons species intermingled before disappearing. After a few minutes, the stands begin to empty as the tournament concludes and preparations for the matching ceremony begin.

I find Draven talking to Eagan. "You fought well, Eagan. Thank you for your strength and skill," Draven tells the man, shaking his hand.

"I held back," Eagan says with a small chuckle as he takes his hand back to rub his neck.

Draven helps the man up and claps hands. We part ways and prepare. This should be the most joyous night for my brother and sister. I hope soon I can set aside my jealousy by finding my own mate.

Tiamat

THIS IS IT, the moment I have been waiting for. I feel giddy and nervous along with excitement. I stare at my mother in her all silver and blue dress. It fits her like a glove with a satin bodice and mermaid train. Mother can rock anything she wears though.

I take a seat with my mother, mother-in-law, and my sister Luna looking at the dress Oberon has sent me. It's a long flowing dress oddly enough made of elvish silk and mithril. The mithril is super light and strong. The king obviously knows my family well and gifts me armor meant for a warrior queen.

It takes both moms' and a lot of luck to get me into this multi-piece of artwork. He went as far as to give me silken wings that attach to my fingertips. We fasten the bodice in place and I feel incredibly beautiful. The bodice itself resembles the scales of my dragon's under-belly. I stretch my arms out several times watching the silken wings flare out with the help of Gisella's Dragons magic.

My mother comes forward with tears in her eyes. "My baby is all grown up." Mom says softly. "I have one last thing to give you as a wedding present. May it serve you well." My mother pulls her ruby crown out of the velvet bag. "This was the crown worn by the Blood Queen herself. You are her last female descendant, therefore I pass it down to you." Mom gently places it upon my head, careful not to mess my hair up.

"Thank you, mother," I kiss both of my mother's cheeks before she applies her signature blood-red lipstick on my lips.

My eyes move towards Gisella and she's smiling. She chose a gown that was also a nod to her Dragon. It's a full length evening gown made from satin and the same bronze-gold color of her scales. She chose to have an embroidered bodice that looks similar to her scales.

"Am I ready mom?" I smile watching her, waiting for her assessment.

"My sweet girl, you look stunning. You are more than ready." She approaches and kisses me on the cheek. "Ready to join my family in name, for you are already part of my heart," Gisella tells me with tears trickling down her face and disappearing before they drop off her chin. I wasn't prepared for that response as I can't find the words and go to hug her tightly. Her Dragoness croons with my Dragoness as we bond.

"You need not say anything," she says. "I know what's in your heart and you will make a great wife, mother, and Queen for I saw it in my dreams last night," Gisella tells me with a bright smile gracing her beautiful face.

My jaw goes slack slightly at her confession, "I don't know what to say, mom."

"Dear girl, don't worry about the future. Enjoy tonight and welcome home," Gisella tells me kissing my forehead. She backs up two steps then bows slightly.

I NOD my head and finish dressing with minimal makeup and no shoes. I guess I am as ready as I'll ever be. We hear the music start and both moms' leave swiftly to take their places. My maid of honor Luna gives me two thumbs up and tells me I've got this. She moves to the door that leads into the grand ballroom where I will be entering from.

"Count to thirty the music will change then it's your turn," Luna says before scooting out the door, leaving me with a wink and my thoughts.

I take a final sip of the blood and vodka my mother left me to steel my nerves. This is going to be a larger display of power than I'm used to letting others see. I lay my bare hand on the door listening for the change in music.

The minute it happens I start dropping the temperature in the ballroom. I use my arctic winds to push the doors open allowing me to exit. My eyes are that of my dragon as I summon my frost flames into my hands. Every step coats the floor in ice, each row I pass receives a coating of frost. At home I'm called the Winter Princess, here too they shall know my name. I raise my hands flaring the silken wings, I stop on my mark waiting to be retrieved by my brother.

Ladon steps out from the wing of the great room decorated with stained glass of dragons. His face is one I haven't seen before, he's looking at me as if I am an angel. I try to hold it together but it is difficult right now but push my feelings down and I gladly accept his hand as he walks me down the frosted isle.

I look forward finally and see my betrothed standing at the top of the steps in an all white tuxedo and bronze tie. His hair is braided back and into a bun and his beard is trimmed up nicely. He looks absolutely dashing and he is to be *mine.*

My steps never falter but my breath becomes quicker as we approach. Draven reaches for my hand but I don't accept it quite yet. Ladon turns me to him with my hands in his.

"I will always be with you no matter how near or far you are sister," he tells me, kisses my cheeks, and takes his place by Draven.

Luna is waiting for me as I walk up one more step to stand before Draven. I smile at him brightly seeing his eyes twinkle to that of his dragon and back. I look to my left and see a man who closely resembles Draven but not entirely, it must be his grandfather, the previous king. He bows gently then motions to the opposite side of the altar. My Grandfather slowly makes his appearance leaving a coating of frost in his wake.

"Hello granddaughter, I am happy to be presiding over you two today." Nicodeamus says as he lowers his arm inviting the attendants to sit. "It is my honor to join the Stormbringer Kingdom tonight for this momentous event." He smiles gently at me then looks back over the room. "We bring together tonight two great bloodlines and two powerful kingdoms."

From the sidelines both of our fathers come forth with ceremonial blades. Each blade on a pillow, our fathers' go to opposite children and stand beside us. "In the days of old potential mates would trade scales to see if they were meant to be." Nicodeamus smiles as he looks at Draven and I before addressing the room again. "My Grand-daughter and her betrothed upon meeting formally performed the scale ceremony. The exchanged scales live and thrive on their new hosts proving they are true mates."

Nicodeamus motions to us to show the crowd the living scales on our chests. I watch Draven intently as he unbuttons his shirt, each button seems to move in slow motion. Every movement has my Dragoness on edge as we get to see more of his flesh. Finally, Draven has his shirt open and untucked and he shows the room his left pec where my silver-white scale lives.

He turns back to my grandfather as he rebuttons his shirt and smiles at him. "There's only two things these two haven't done to finalize their union." Nicodeamus smirks. "One happens behind closed doors, and the other is the sharing of blood. There's one of two ways it can be done, with the ceremonial blades or with mating bites."

Nicodeamus's eyes shift to that of his Dragon at the mention of the bites.

My eyes drift to the blades before us then up to Draven and my Dragoness is pushing me hard to complete the next step in bonding. ***Bite him, taste him, make him ours***. She demands of me, I smile sweetly at Draven as I open my mouth, slowly my canines descend. My eyes shift to that of my Dragoness as I move towards him.

My Dragoness makes her crooning noise as we approach and I watch the scales race over Draven's exposed flesh. Draven's eyes shift to that of his Dragon and his mouth opens revealing his canines. His Dragon must sense the power within me because he doesn't make the first move.

Slowly I run my nose under his jaw and down his throat. My hot breath washing over his skin. Extending a finger I shift my nail to my talon and cut free the top few buttons of his shirt. Gently I push the offending cloth out of the way as I run my lips over the thick muscle between his shoulder and neck.

Bite him, make him ours. My Dragoness hisses in my mind. I open my mouth slowly and rest my canines over his flesh. I feel his hand come to rest at the back of my neck. My breaths are coming in pants as anticipation builds within me. I feel the hum of power radiating within Draven. Gently he starts to massage the muscles in my neck telling me in his own way that he's ready. He pulls me gently close to him trying to give me the security

I need. I bite him quickly, sinking my canines deeply into his muscle.

He hisses softly from the sting of my canines breaking through his flesh. The hot metallic tang of his blood fills my mouth and I begin to get flashes of his life. His hopes and fears, most importantly his dreams. I close my eyes reveling in the feeling of him, his love for me knows no bounds. I feel the power of his infinite love, and it brings me comfort.

His lips caress the side of my neck and trail to my shoulder slowly, almost hesitantly. Carefully I tilt my head to the side still latched onto him. My hand slides up his chest to caress the side of his neck. Lightly I pull his face to my shoulder holding him there encouraging him to bite me. The sweet sting of pain washes over me as his canines sink deeply into my flesh. My power hums beneath the surface and slowly washes over both of us covering us in a thin layer of frost.

His Dragon croons to mine as we stand locked in our embrace. Slowly I withdraw my canines from his muscle and lick the wounds, sealing them. Draven still drinks deeply as his hands roughly caress my sides. His beast rumbles just before he releases my shoulder. Gently he licks the wounds sealing them then hugs me to him tightly. Our gathered families as well as friends erupt in cheers as I look up to him and kiss his lips gently.

Nicodeamus smiles broadly as he raises his hand to get the crowd under control. "Blood and scales have been exchanged; their bond once fully complete shall run deeper than the deepest ocean." Nicodeamus steps forward and kisses mine and Draven's foreheads then backs up. "By the power vested in me, by birthright, I now pronounce you Prince and Princess Draven Storm-bringer, heirs' of the Stormbringer Kingdom." Cheers erupt again except this time Draven and I run down the aisle and out of the room to the banquet hall.

FIFTEEN

TIAMAT

I choose to remain glued to Draven's side as we enter the banquet hall. His extended family has arrived as well as dignitaries from around the world for our big day. Draven ushers me to our seats to start the receiving line for the reception. Carefully my beloved mate adjusts my crown and kisses my lips reverently. I'm almost constantly purring being in contact with him. I can't help it, but I keep looking at our joined hands and then back to our scales.

Make him ours completely... My Dragoness hisses in the back of my mind. Her statement puzzles me, I have his scale, tasted his blood and bare his mark and his name. What else could there be?

Draven looks at me concerned. "My love, are you ok?" He says as he touches my cheek with the backs of his knuckles.

I smile before answering. "My Dragoness is confusing me again." I shake my head lightly. "She wants me to make you ours completely." I shrug my shoulders then look to my twin who's choking on his drink. "I'm not understanding what she's talking about, beloved." I watch Draven's eyes shift to his beast and I feel mesmerized by his gaze.

Draven breaks eye contact first then leans in to whisper in my ear. "She's talking about what comes after the party, my love." He pulls back slowly waiting for me to connect the dots.

I swallow hard and feel the tingles of anticipation move through me. At this point, Gisella brings me a glass of wine, and Austin gives Draven a beer.

"How are you holding up, Tia?" Gisella asks me.

Carefully I stand and accept my glass of wine then lightly place my hand on Gisella's elbow hoping she gets the hint. She smiles understanding that I need her and she makes an excuse for both of us to leave for a moment. Gisella had excellent timing as I look over my shoulder seeing Draven's brothers' and cousins' join him and their father in conversation. Once we are out of earshot of the boys I sigh softly.

"I'm doing as well as a virgin on her wedding night can possibly do," I say frankly. "My Dragoness is becoming quite demanding and I think she may bring on our heat early. She's quite interested in Draven's Drake."

Gisella smiles knowingly, "I wouldn't be shocked if she

does just that." She motions to the party goers. "The combined scent of the two of you is driving some of the attendees crazy."

I blush at Gisella's words then tilt my head at her. "Will we be allowed to have our sense of smell back soon?" I ask curiously.

Gisella smirks as she motions to her mage then winks at me. I draw in a deep breath and feel my canines descend almost immediately.

"Wow...yeah, I see what you mean." I close my eyes reveling in the scent my mate is giving off. I feel Draven's presence at my back as his hands rest on my hips. I lean back against Draven feeling his strength and the rumblings of his beast trying to soothe me.

"Sweet girl I am curious to see what gifts you will gain from each other. I shall leave you two to speak for a moment but please try to return to the party," she tells me with a side smile.

"Why wouldn't we return to the party?" I ask Draven as I turn around to face him chest to chest and I catch a whiff of his scent now stronger than before. Draven's eyes shift to that of his Dragon and the air around us becomes a little warmer.

"I think you know why, my love," he tells me with a little growl and his voice that turns my bones liquid.

"My Dragoness and I are both in agreement about tonight. I cannot wait to be yours," I tell him as I lean forward to kiss his lips. He breaks off the kiss too early to my dismay.

"My love, if we do not control ourselves for the rest of this evening we may wind up turning our dignitaries and friends into mindless sex beasts," he says with a chuckle and quickly pushes his hands down grabbing my ass pulling me into his hips.

Shit.

"That's for being a good girl, I'd love to see what happens when you're a bad girl," then he takes my hand and walks me back into the party.

Time seems to be going slowly for my liking. My Dragoness is becoming restless in anticipation of our mating tonight. It's getting to the point that I am almost whining.

"Daughter, why don't we take a spin on the dance floor?" Father asks me. " Draven, you don't mind, do you son?"

"No sir, please come back soon though. We are about to wrap up for the evening," he says with a wink.

"I wouldn't dream of it son," Father says to Draven before whisking me off to the dance floor.

Father looks over to the orchestra conductor and raises his hand. Immediately the music changes to *"Swan Lake by Tchaikovsky."* It was the same song Dad and I danced to for my coming of age party. It's one of the more lively waltzes. Dad tends to like to pick me up by my waist and spin me in the air for some of the fancy turns. He has me laughing hysterically at his antics, I know he's trying to settle my nerves. "Thank you, daddy, for always being there and keeping me safe." I lay my head on my father's chest as we dance.

"Are you truly happy Tia?" He smiles looking down at me briefly as we dance.

"I am Daddy, I just wish I had a better idea of what's expected of me later...you know." I blush furiously, then start to laugh feeling how uncomfortable my father is with the subject.

Father clears his throat. "About that, um...your Dragoness will guide you, baby girl. Trust her judgment and try not to rip the poor man to shreds with your talons." Dad says with a smile. I know in my heart he's more worried about Draven's safety than my own.

I see Austin approach behind my father and tap him on the shoulder. "Mind if I get a few minutes with my new daughter, brother?" Father bows lightly to Austin then kisses my cheek. Gently Austin takes my father's place and the song changes to *"Claire De Lune by Debussy."*

We move in time with the music and I discover my new dad is a great dance partner. "I was shocked when you put my son's safety and happiness before your own desires. Draven is blessed to have such a loving and thoughtful mate." Austin says with a smile.

I can't help but giggle a little bit. "It's far easier for me to bring winter here for me than for summer to happen in Siberia." I smile broadly settling into our dance.

"That is true...we don't get much snow here but I'm sure with the Winter Princess here that will change," Austin says with a playful smirk. I see where Draven gets his suave personality from.

"The Summer Chalet honestly isn't terribly far. I made it here in six hours from there and they get a decent snowstorm or two." I am happy to be fully accepted by Draven's parents.

"Will you get homesick Tia?" Austin asks cautiously.

"It's bound to happen, but it's nice to be able to see the world and enjoy the simple comforts of even a dance with someone that's not related to me." I look over to my twin who happens to have a small flock of females hanging on his every word.

"My brother won't be leaving the Stormbringer Kingdom anytime soon. He has a lot more training and I'm sure he's looking for his Mrs. Kraus." Austin and I share a hearty laugh at my poor brother's expense. The song ends and Austin escorts me back to Draven.

I extend both hands to Draven and grip his offered hands tightly. I look up into his eyes and see the hunger there. His scent becomes thick and intoxicating. I feel my body flush in response to his scent. If I didn't know better I think my Dragoness has gone completely mad. She's pushing us to go into heat again, she wants hatchlings more than anything.

I shake my head trying to clear my thoughts as Draven starts to lead us out of the banquet hall. He pauses by the kitchen and places an order to be brought to us. Carefully Draven tucks me into his side as we briskly walk down the hall to his room. He kicks the door open then bends down and scoops me up into his arms and carries me across the threshold.

SIXTEEN

DRAVEN

I can't believe she is mine, my mate, my true love, mine to cherish for the end of time. Tia's Dragoness is calling to me like a siren in the night and yet her innocence makes me stop and think rationally.

I need to slow down and take my time to savor her even if her scent is driving me mad. I know she is ready for this but I am not ready to end her taunting quite yet.

I shut the door behind me and place her gently on the floor then pin her against the wall with my lips alone. I keep my hands above my head and allow her to explore me and enjoy what she has been denied for so long.

Tia sucks in a deep breath as she begins touching my torso and chest tentatively. I have little tingles cascading throughout my body and my pants become too tight, all too fast.

I hold back on burning my clothes off right that moment, I don't want to scare the poor woman. My beast growls as she stops kissing me and she begins unbuttoning my shirt slowly. It's agonizing and I am mesmerized by her movements.

She darts her tongue out to wet her lips and I cover her mouth with mine once more, being torn between patience and impatience. We've both waited too long, it's as if this is all a dream.

I break off the kiss and stand straight up allowing her to move freely to do what she wishes to me. I'll always let her play because this relationship is going to be built on mutual respect. Tia eyes my exposed torso and moves her head to me, licking me from navel to chest. When she stops and peeks up at me I see her Dragoness in her eyes making me all the hungrier.

"My love, we need to slow down. I want you to do everything you want to do and explore," I say grabbing her hands and placing my forehead on hers.

"I want whatever everything is, *now*," she responds with a growl. Her canines descend punctuating her impatience.

"I can see you are impatient and that your Dragoness is ready but I need to make sure you are ready as well," I say cautiously, honestly I truly believe her Dragoness is bigger and stronger than my Drake.

"Whatever you think is best, mate," she says with a small huff and a slight snarl.

"Let's snack and drink, I smell food and spotted a bottle of Ice Wine on the way in," I offer motioning to my table with our treats.

FIVE BOTTLES OF ICE WINE, two plates of strawberries and other assorted fruits with melted chocolate. I think this was all our mom's doing, they want what's best for Tia. I roll my eyes internally and pop the top on the wine, pour some into the flutes and hand one to Tia.

"To us, my love," I toast.

"To us." She says softly.

We clink glasses, put them down and go for the fruits and chocolate. I feed Tia the largest strawberry with chocolate on it. Some chocolate stays around the corners of her mouth so I take it upon myself to clean her up and lick it off. I am greeted in return by a throaty growl.

"Draven, please, whatever you are doing is torturous. Do what you wish to me and let's enjoy the evening," she pants.

"I have so much more in store for you, my love. After tonight, we will travel for our honeymoon to an island off of Alaska. There's a small cottage your father's friend Ellis uses in the winter." I smile just before I trail kisses along her jaw.

"We can fly whenever, wherever and not be interrupted for royal duties. We can enjoy each other for a whole week and indulge in anything and everything you want."

I punctuate each sentence with a kiss. "We can visit the Winter Palace as well as the Summer Chalet on the way back here.

"I think I am beginning to understand why you won't be able to hide from me, Draven." Her smile turns feral as she looks at me with a new hunger in her eyes. "My Dragoness is in the back of my head pushing me to claim you. Don't make me wait too much longer," she says with a smirk. "I need to get this dress off and carefully. I will change into something more comfortable, is your bathroom behind you?"

"Yes, it is." I sweep my hand in the direction she needs to go.

"Good, and a shower will help too, I think," she tells me as she flows into my bathroom.

I GROAN and go to adjust my pants, damn it she is going to kill me. Here I thought I had her on the brink but she has me on a thread so thin it could snap in a moment. I hear the shower starting and a warm trickle as I feel her hands on my body as if she's in front of me.

I groan inwardly as I adjust my cock for the umpteenth time in the last hour. Tia starts singing in the shower and it's like a siren's call. My Dragon is urging me to go to her. Bracing my hands on the table I hang my head trying to control my breathing.

Her scent drifts to me and its changing from earlier. If I didn't know better I'd think her Dragoness was bringing on a second heat just for me. "Tia, come on out my love," I tell her, grabbing a towel to wrap her up in.

Her nakedness makes me growl in appreciation but I must show some restraint. So I tend to drying her off starting from her face and hair moving down slowly letting her enjoy the feel of my hands touching her everywhere.

Her Dragoness is emitting a throaty rumble in response. I watch her arms closely as they shift slightly into her scales.

"Let's drink some champagne and I will finish drying you off in the bedroom," I tell her.

We both finish our glasses, set them down and I lead her next to my bed. The king sized bed is plush and filled with soft pillows that I think she will like, after all what's mine is hers now. I back her legs up to the bed and kneel to finish drying her by starting at her feet.

As I dry her I blow hot air against her skin, receiving her hands in my long hair and a purr. The scent she is putting off now is even stronger than it was before, thick rain surrounds me as I get closer to her center. I test the waters and lick her slit just once quickly and pull away but she grabs my head and places me back where I was.

I'm going to go mad with her on my tongue as I push in and out then move in circles, not being very delicate. I lay her down on the bed using my hands on her torso, not using my body as I want but with my mouth right where it is.

"Draven...please..." She whines begging me to finish what I started.

I mumble 'no' but contradict it by slipping my tongue a little further and give her a full lick. Her legs jerk up and I place them over my shoulders. I hear tearing on the bed and realize she has shifted to her gauntlets. She's losing control and on the edge of oblivion so I move at a more rapid pace, grabbing her hips pushing her into me more.

Tia moans out in pleasure as her first orgasm racks her body, her legs holding tightly to my head. I smile, let her relax as do I but my urge to mate with her completely is on the brink of driving me insane and I don't wish to hurt her.

Tiamat

GODS this man is gifted with his mouth and taunting. My breathing evens out and I reach for Draven to drag him up my body and have him between my thighs. His weight upon me is like a warm blanket making me feel safe and secure. Without hesitation my hands thread through his hair as his lips crash down upon mine.

Draven moves up my body till I feel something hard yet soft gently prodding at my entrance. He groans softly.

"You're so wet baby.. I'll be gentle." He says as he kisses my lips softly.

He slowly rocks forward, inching his member deeper within me. The girth of his shaft's head stretches me slowly. He slowly withdraws what little he got in to push further in the next time. This push he finds a barrier, softly I whine and squirm because of the pressure I'm experiencing.

Draven has a brilliant idea and bites me again over my mating mark sending me off the deep end. I cry out feeling my abdomen tense and almost quiver just before he pushes forward past the barrier.

The pain mixed with pleasure causes my arms to shift to my gauntlets. What little mental fortitude I have left I throw my arms out to the side digging my talons into the mattress. The sound of fabric ripping causes Draven to lift his head and look at what I've done.

My Dragoness is on the surface as my facial plates shift and realign several times. Tiny scales emerge between my breasts on my sternum. Draven starts to move slowly sending ripples of intense pleasure through me. I carefully shift my hands back and paw at his back pulling him towards me more.

His long slow strokes drive me to my peak again slowly. My abdomen is tightening and tingles move throughout my body, Draven pulls my leg up higher driving himself in deeper. I cry out as my orgasm rips through me, I feel my muscles pulsing around his shaft. Instinctually I reach up and bite Draven over his mating mark. He howls out as his orgasm rips through him and he buries himself deep within me. I feel his shaft pulsing deep within me, he grunts and bites my mating mark again.

His second bite sends me over the edge again. Suddenly I start to feel lightheaded and Draven's movements become uncoordinated. I watch him fall to the side and his eyes roll back in his head. Try to roll over to him and my body is unresponsive, I can't even lift my head at this point. Just before things go dark there a man standing over me with a syringe in his hands.

SEVENTEEN

DRAVEN

I put my hand to my head rubbing it tenderly, goddamnit my head feels like it's exploding. What the hell happened? I don't remember getting hit in the head by a flying hammer. It was my mating night with Tia.

Tia!

I rub my eyes furiously trying to wake up. Quickly I reach out patting the bed trying to find Tiamat. Quickly I roll to the side looking around the room for her. The evidence of our mating is on the bed as well as the thick scent that tells me she was starting her heat sometime last night. I race around my room looking for her when I catch a third scent in the room. My beast growls because the scent is on the bed near where Tia was.

"Mother, you may want to help me before I do something stupid. Come to my room please, fast! " I reach out through the bond, panicking.

Mom doesn't respond but I know she'll be here. My mind starts racing as the events from last night are blurred. I remember moving in on Tia and watching her fall apart for me but I can't remember anything else. I pinch the bridge of my nose. Did she go hunting for an apex predator for me?

No, she would have left a note I'm sure! I take off to my balcony and search the sky for her or Ladon but nothing. Maybe they're in an ice sleep and she's terrified of me now for what I can't remember. Did I hurt her and she hates me?

What went wrong when it was going so incredibly right? I swear if I didn't know better her Dragoness was on the verge of a heart cycle. Could we have hatchlings and I not know? A knock sounds at the door and I run back to let my mother in.

"Son, what's wrong? I feel you panicking," she says worriedly.

"Tia, she's not here, I can't find her!" I throw my arms open wide and spin slightly.

"What do you mean, Draven? Speak slowly please." My mother questions softly.

"I remember the beginning of our night, I remember both of us finishing." I run my hands down my face. "*How can I not know where she is?*" I ask, going into a panic.

"Something isn't right. What did you eat and drink last night?" Mother starts walking around the room. "We all had the same things at dinner and everyone else is fine," mom says.

"We had a couple of bottles of champagne and a tray of treats. I figured both moms' brought them as a gift for us," I say, still agitated.

"We would never enter your nest especially on your mating night.," she says quietly with a hiss. "Someone was here...," she trails off letting her mage use his magic to explore the area of my room. "Draven, you need to step out to the balcony. I will call your dad to help me, okay?" She says with an awkward smile.

I nod my head though I know she is hiding something. Who else would have dropped the drinks and food off? A dignitary by chance, or a friend did? My head is exploding as I sit on the edge of the bed that held the best night of my life. I feel cold, my chest aches as I rub my chest next to Tia's scale. Maybe I can reach out to her.

"Tia, my love, where are you? I am worried sick." I concentrate as hard as I can, I can feel her, but not where she is.

After several moments I only hear silence which only makes my stomach drop further. I hear other footsteps coming towards my room and the door opens once more. Dad, Alaric, Aurora and Marco all come in. What the fuck?

"Draven, step out to the balcony, son," dad tells me.

I almost question him but at this point I'm ready to explode and shift. "Someone *please* explain to me what the hell is happening?" I all but roar out as I step out of my room.

"Your mother thinks someone has taken advantage of us not having the Mages' closer," dad says tentatively.

"I think you've been drugged," she says, "and by the smell of this bottle...it's true. I think someone took Tia," she says cautiously.

"They did *what*?" I say as my anger gets the better of me and I flip my lid shifting.

I take off to the sky in a hurry roaring out my anger with lighting and flames. I turn around to see my family trying to console Tia's parents. I think they're in shock but soon it will be replaced with anger. I blow fire in every which direction and finally let out my battle cry notifying the entire kingdom that we are in full alert. We will go on lockdown until Tia is found and so help me, I will rip anyone to shreds who has taken liberties to lay a hand on her.

I see only red releasing another wave of fire with a second battle cry. Ladon answers my call first then his guard Marco, a massive Black Dragon. The three of us take off for the Hotel Darkfang to the north where I know we can find out any information about anyone, anywhere in the world.

Someone will pay for their idiocy and it will be with their life.

WE ALL LAND with our clothes intact as we shift to our human forms. I am on the rampage, though I know I need to take it easy at first so I don't rip this place down to the ground. Who am I kidding, I want to rip everyone I see in half and light this place up.

"I heard our parents' call. We will find her," Ladon tells me calmly although I know he is anything but. "We'll tear anyone in our way to pieces," he says with venom in his voice.

"M'lord, I have your back. We will find your mate, this I swear to you," Ladon's guard, Marco tells me.

I nod unable to say anything without fire erupting from my mouth. I shove the front doors open with a bang, ignoring the hostess and go straight to the mercenary room. You can buy anyone there to do dirty work or otherwise. I would know the best as it's my job in secret to assassinate...go in stealth and wipe out anyone in my way. Now is no different with the exception that I am not going in quietly.

The three of us walk in and begin hunting for the moth-erfucker who crossed me and my family. There be hell to pay and heads will roll.

EPILOGUE

Sylvos

WE'VE BEEN TRACKING THIS FEMALE FOR YEARS. Finally she's within our grasp and easy to access. We had to wait for her to take a mate for the connection to her twin to be weakened to the point he wouldn't sense everything from her.

Replacing some of the staff with our Mages' was easier than I ever anticipated. With all the preparations for not one but then a second mating ceremony, they practically handed her to us. Don't even get me started about the tournament that they decided to throw, their castle was handed to us on a silver platter. Dax got impatient and tried taking her at the dance, he didn't expect her to resist his charm.

Alkor and Draziel are on their way back with the female now. Such an exciting time for us, we finally have a descendant of the Blood Queen. We could have easily stolen Aurora, but she was more mutt than dragon. Her daughter Tiamat I'm sure is almost a complete throw back to the Blood Queen. Thankfully she's still young enough she hasn't come into her full powers yet. I have plans to mold her and poison her mind. I'll turn her against her own people and destroy all shifters.

My eyes shift to the dark elves I have working for me, yes they will be next to be disposed of. I look back over the scrolls studying the records of the Blood Queen's powers. I hope that my prize is ripe and ready to be bred, I have an enslaved Black Dragon that would be perfect for her.

"Boss?" Jaden says cautiously.

"What do you need? Don't you see I'm busy?" I motion to all of the scrolls in front of me.

"I'm just concerned about bringing an enraged Drag-oness here boss. How long will she sleep for?" Jaden wrings his hands showing how frightened he actually is.

I roll my eyes then move around the table towards him. "I don't pay you to think. Besides, the elves assure me the mix of valerian root, paralysis potion and sleep potion will keep her under as long as we keep dosing her." I motion to the dark elves working in the lab off to my right.

"They've been in the business of killing and poisoning for longer than most species." I nod lightly to Azriel, the leader of the dark elves. "I have full confidence in their abilities."

. . .

THE ROAR of the Black Dragon, Zefavion, announces he's returned with my precious cargo. We emerge from our lab to meet him in the courtyard. Jaden pushes the gurney out with him behind me. Alkor and Draziel slide off of Zefavion's back and move to his taloned hand. Slowly he reveals his cargo, my cargo appears intact on initial inspection.

Jaden goes to remove the girl from Zefavion's hand and he growls at him protectively, apparently the Dragoness is about to go into heat. Perfect...Draziel hits Zefavion in the nose with a bolt of energy to remind him who his master is. Once the girl is loaded we roll her back inside.

"Did you run into any difficulties Alkor?" I look up briefly from the girl as I examine her and check her vitals.

"No, I knocked her and her mate out, I had to triple the dose to make it effective." He states plainly.

"Oh? Triple the dose you say? Hmm.. I'll need to run DNA testing on her and regular blood work to determine the most effective dose for her." I motion to the briefcase on the table by the door. "Your fee is there, thank you for your service."

Alkor walks over and grabs the briefcase. "You know how to find me, should you need me again," he says, turning away leaving swiftly.

I draw several vials of blood from the girl and start setting them into the different machines to run the battery of tests. I sip at my coffee watching the different tests run, waiting impatiently for the results. Over the next hour I assess her vitals and get measurements. I take note of a single bronze scale on her chest as well as two bites on her right shoulder. The bites are fresh and I suspect the mating has been finalized.

The first of the machines finish their tests so I walk over to look over the results. To be honest I am quite shocked to see the mix in her bloodline. All these years I was under the impression that the species didn't interbreed but here's this female blowing the theory out of the water.

By the looks of it, she is forty percent Platinum Dragon, the rarest of all dragons. Glacial and Silver Dragon are each at twenty five percent. I'm shocked to see that her mother's Lycan bloodline is only at ten percent. Oddly enough there's an anomaly at five percent that seems to be that of a Gold Dragon. That can't be right, so I ignore the last five percent.

The next test completes and her metabolism is far faster than the average Dragoness, it must be from the Lycan heritage. I start to calculate the dosage of the next elixir for her based off of body weight and the test results.

I watch the scales start to ripple under her flesh and she murmurs the name **Draven** softly. There's a burst of power that emanates from her as soon as she speaks his name.

My female assistant finishes the rest of her examination and relays to me that the Dragoness has been bred. This is horrible news, as far as my research goes they are fully bonded, perhaps as long as I keep her sedated he won't find her. If that works I don't have to worry about some angry Drake trying to rain fire down on my facility. I still have six more tests to wait on so I return to my desk. I watch my assistant hook up the IV drip to the female to keep her under.

~Hotel Darkfang~
Alkor

WHAT A FUCKED up situation I got myself into this time. The things I let my lover Draziel talk me into. With this last job we can buy our freedom and get away from these filthy Blood Mages. Human scum think that tampering with the natural order of things is the way to go.

I navigate my way to the bar where all of our meetings take place. This particular room in the Hotel Darkfang is for mercenaries and traders alike. Slowly I raise my eyes to the jobs board and look to see what's available. Not many speak Dark Elf so the card with the job I just completed is still hanging in place on the cork board.

I order a mug of mazte and wait for my next contact to arrive. Damn Black Dragons, the only good Black Dragon is an enslaved one. My mazte arrives and I sip at it slowly savoring its flavor. Now I just have to wait to either get hired again or figure out how to escape with my lover undetected from this plane of existence.

I feel the presence of three newcomers in the room but pay little mind to them. They are not important, only my drink and my escape. That poor girl's life will be miserable once that Black Dragon gets a hold of her. They might keep her drugged for the rest of her life. Who knows but I truly don't care anymore, not my problem.

I drink the last bit of my drink, pay the bill and begin to take my leave. I throw my hood up over my head and rise from my chair. I walk a few steps before bumping into the man with long dark hair.

"Watch it, asshole," I bark out.

"Pardon me, who the *fuck* do you think you are?" the man yells back at me.

I turn around and get a good look at him. Suddenly the man goes rigid and a pulse of power can be felt from the direction of the female's location. Scales ripple over his face and his eyes shift to his Dragon's as he stares at me. Son of a bitch, it looks like I really messed up this time.

"Where is she? I smell her on you, you *pathetic* piece of shit!" He grips my shirt and holds firm. "Speak now or I will gut you where you stand!" He yells at me as my arms are grabbed by the other two men. I should have known better than to take this blasted job.

"You will not find her, she is to be useful to her new owner," I tell him without revealing any details of the job. I was paid for my silence after all but what good is that if I am dead?

"You're about to be useful to me, Dark Elf. I will start by plucking out one of your eyes with my talons then rip out your innards while you still live," he says threatening me with his eyes that of his dragon.

The air becomes suffocating as his body begins to shift and everyone in the room leaves. The grip on my arms becomes tighter. "That is my *sister* and his *mate* you are speaking about," the blonde male says venomously in my ear. His hands become ice cold on my skin causing my muscles to spasm.

The blonde takes both of my arms and the third person has black scales move over his flesh. A fucking Black Dragon, just my damn luck. I hear the rumble of his Dragon and then he spits on me. My flesh starts to bubble and burn as his acid burns my skin. I scream out in pain till the blonde stops the burning.

"Tell me where she is or I will end you here and now in a pile of ash," the dark headed one says as he paces back and forth trying to control himself.

"I only know that I was hired to retrieve a descendant of the Blood Queen, to have access to her. I was told to abduct her and return back to base," I offer up. I hear an angry rumble from the dark haired one so I continue. "He is looking for a specific DNA pattern, her brother here is not enough of a descendant to have qualified for the man's needs."

"What do you mean...*needs*?" the dark haired one says. I've connected the dots and now know it's her mate. I am dead, I might as well give them everything they need to know. It's either I die at their hands, or by Sylvos.

I raise a single white eyebrow knowing my death is imminent now. "She is to be a breeder. There's a Black Dragon Drake slave that bears the markers for the Abyssal Black Dragon lines." I smirk watching the information sink in deeply. "Sylvos is trying to breed a war-machine, the ultimate beast immune to every weapon ever created."

Slowly I look at the two males. "She signed her own abduction warrant by showing she is clearly immune to Bronze Dragon lighting, as well as Phoenix fire. I highly doubt this one," I motion with my head to her brother behind me, "would survive such a test. I hear fried Dragons are divine by the way."

"To think she hasn't even come into her full power yet!" I start to laugh, being on the brink of death will do that to you. "I doubt Sylvos has a clue as to how powerful she'll become!" I laugh insanely. "That beast of a mother of hers? Not even close to being on the same level as her daughter," I say as I shake my head slowly with a twisted smile playing upon my lips.

I'm released and the three men's faces before me are twisted in different stages of rage and disbelief. I wonder who is going to snap first and end my life? Will it be the defective brother? The mate with the anger issues, Or the third man that I can't quite figure out as of yet.

"You will take us to her, or you will die. Do you understand that?" the older hybrid threatens me.

"If I die, You won't find her... Your bond is new and fragile yet," I offer then tilt my head to the side watching them.

"How the *fuck* do you know that?" the so-called mate asks.

"Easy, she's in heat. If you sealed the deal, or hit the mark the heat would be over lover boy..." I smirk looking at him. I'm rushed by the mate but he's stopped by the older one.

Unfortunately for me I get decked in the face by the defective brother and go down to one knee. "Look I would love to sit here and banter with the lot of you but I am going to take my leave now." I say as I try to get up to leave.

"You will not go anywhere...but to be trapped here on earth without a chance of resurrection.." The older one says as he smirks.

I am suffocating slowly and immobile. What is happening to me? I reach up to my throat to stop the invisible force but nothing. I drop to the floor unable to draw breath. An aura surrounds me as the Black Dragons eyes glow as he stares at me..

"You will stay in a frozen afterlife, I hope you enjoy it," the older one tells me.

I am encased in frost up to my shoulders before my throat is sliced open slowly and I begin to bleed out. My life force is draining and the last thing I can think of is to taunt them as my airway opens momentarily. "She will be a good ride."

Draven

LADON FINISHES ENCASING the filthy piece of shit in ice. No one will ever breach that block now. I love that he is on display with a blood fountain as a warning to all who wants to fuck with me or my mate.

"Let's go. Thanks for the assist, Marco." I say, trying to calm down and focus on the power surge I felt from Tia. I know it was her and I am dying on the inside.

Marco looks between Ladon and I and then he smirks. "I believe that blast is the start of her ascension. Or possibly she's with hatchling?" He raises his eyebrows looking at me and it hits home.

Dread settles in the pit of my stomach as I ponder what Marco has suggested. What would happen to a hatchling if she ascends at the same time? I look to Ladon who has the same look of shock on his face as I do. "Can you question your parents what the outcome may be? Or even your grandfather?" My emotions are a disaster as I ponder what could be happening to my mate. I know the direction I sensed the power surge from and I'm anxious to take flight.

Ladon smiles and gives me two thumbs up. "Grandpa said that as long as she's not far along the ascension will not harm the babies." Ladon smiles and shrugs his shoulders. Armed with this good news I can relax a little and focus on finding Tia instead of panicking.

We leave the Hotel Darkfang and take to the skies. I will find her, rescue her and make sure she and my potential hatchlings are safe. Marco suggests through the bond to stop at one of his family's estates and use some of their surveillance equipment there. We can rest and feed before heading back out again in search of Tia. We fly higher and higher up the side of a mountain in northern Africa till we reach a lair on a plateau.

The lair is over five thousand square feet with beds, living space and filled with the best technology known to man or supernatural. We will use whatever means necessary to pinpoint where I felt her and I will tear down the entire country looking for her.

I head back to one of the rooms to get changed out of my old clothes. I put on new briefs and lounge pants, it's time to get down to business. The guys must be getting set up as well because I hear the machines starting up with a low hum.

"What do we have?" I ask.

"The magnitude of the power blast was massive so we should be able to pinpoint the location shortly. I'm waiting for everything to finish powering up," Ladon says in a stern voice.

I know he is panicked like I am since he can sense her as well. It might be that it is more dull now that we have mated, I'm not sure. I get the espresso machine going and realize that Marco isn't here. Where did he take off to? Wandering the lair I find a natural spring running through what must be a meditation room.

I find Marco at the edge of the water meditating, I sit next to him and take a deep breath and touch Tia's scale. My chest hurts, the pain is crushing at times to the point I feel like I cannot breathe. I want to burn the world to ash to find her.

"Draven, I know how you are feeling. I would gladly join you in burning the entire country down to find Tiamat but we have to be careful," Marco says to me now looking at me. "You have to find your center, find her aura in your heart and hold on tight to it. When we get to her and Ladon takes her to safety, then you can go all supernova and blow everything straight to hell."

"I know Marco, but it hurts so damn bad. I want to scream and cry in anger that this happened right under my nose." Roughly I run my fingers through my hair. "Why would anyone want to take her?" I ask no one in particular.

"You have to realize, Draven, she is extremely powerful in her own right and she will only grow stronger with age," Marco explains. "I remember the Blood Queen, I was a hatchling towards the end of her reign. There was nothing stronger than her, she was to be the harbinger of Ragnarok." Marco looks down studying his hands. "I fear that Tiamat will be strong enough to bring about the end of days." He looks up to me completely serious.

"I've seen her shift and I've seen her fight. If she gets any stronger she'll be more powerful than I am," I tell him.

"Yes, that is true. But, she loves you to no end." He smiles and sighs. "You are her forever. If she was awake or able to fight she would be searching for you right now." he says.

"*Draven, Marco!*" The both of us turn around and see Ladon rushing to us. We meet him halfway sensing his urgency.

"I have a brilliant idea!" Ladon says with a smile.

"Speak up!" I urge him.

"We can find her in the astral plane!" Ladon says as if we are both idiots. My eyes go wide in realization and we all rush to the house to prepare. Marco sits off to the side of the living room and waits for us to return.

"Let's go get her, brother," I say with excitement.

We find our center and reach for the thread that is the astral plane. As we meditate the area around us shifts and the bright white of the astral plane opens to us. When we arrive we look around for what feels like forever, eventually we find her Dragoness but no Tia.

Approaching slowly we survey the area we find Tia's Dragoness but don't see her human form anywhere. Suddenly the Dragoness lifts her head suddenly going on the defensive ready to attack anything that comes near her. It takes Ladon's and my dragon's ambling over for her to settle down. Eventually she lifts her wing revealing a sleeping Tiamat snuggled against her side.

"Tia!" Ladon and I say in unison.

Crouching down I look her over slowly. There's no obvious signs of damage that has been done to her. But she refuses to awaken. I try kissing her lips and nuzzling her cheek, nothing is working.

"What is happening, my love? Where are you?" I ask and my beast speaks for me.

"We were abducted and drugged, taken against our will." Tia's Dragoness says angrily, gnashing her teeth. "I want to eat them all one by one until there are bones protruding from my teeth!" Her Dragoness responds to us. Her heavy tail thrashes behind her showing her agitation.

"We will find you, my love. You will come home safe, you are mine," my beast says. "You are a beloved mate, sister, daughter and daughter in law." He says as I thread my fingers through her hair.

Ladon's beast croons, Tia's and mine join in the love fest. After a few minutes we all back up and I hold Tia's body close to mine. I notice my mate's Dragoness has an interesting hue to her flank and a little around her lips extending to her cheeks. I look at my beast and he looks at her and he takes a deep whiff. I watch his pupils dilate to that of an abnormally large size.

"What is this intoxicating smell?" He asks of his own volition.

Ladon's Dragon responds, "She's pregnant, we have to find her **now**."

The Dragoness stands, and approaches my much smaller Drake. Slowly she runs her maw along his and down his neck. The deep rumbling purr coming from the two of them makes my heart ache. My Drake is about three quarters of the size of Tia's Dragoness and is trying his best to curl around her to provide comfort. "Combined we will wake her." My Drake and Tia's Dragoness say as one. "We must protect the hatchlings." My Drake yells in my head as they curl tighter together. The way their scales rub and slide over each other sound like a rattlesnake's rattle. They keep slipping and sliding their necks and tails over each other starting to create arcs of power.

"I haven't witnessed this in a great many years." Marco says in awe of the scene before him.

"What exactly are they doing?" I ask, almost panicking.

"They are going to force Tiamat's ascension and the raw power involved will wake her up almost immediately." No sooner did the words fall from Marco's lips did four more dragons' arrive in the astral plane.

Ladon's Dragon moves to join Tia's and my dragon. Soon after Marco's Dragon and apparently my parents' dragons curl up too. I can't believe what I'm seeing. Shortly after two Ice Dragons round out the pile up. Eventually my parents, Tia's parents as well as her grandfather catch up.

"This hasn't been done in at least a millennium or two. Be prepared for an all out war when Tia wakes up. She will

be fired by her Dragon's desire to protect its babies."
Nicodeamus says with a fire in his voice I've never heard
before.

It's all a waiting game now. Goddess help any innocents
in my mates path. The power I am feeling off the dragons'
could very possibly bring about the end of days.

..... To be continued in Book 2 Hybrid Royals: Destiny
Found

Printed in Great Britain
by Amazon

46974225R00149